RAGGED

SKY

RAGGED

SKY

LAST FLIGHT OF THE SPIRIT WALKER

by

Steve Arnold

Chardon, Ohio, USA

Taylor & Wells Publishing
11525 Taylor-Wells Rd.
Chardon, OH, USA 44024
www.taylor-wells.com

First Print Edition

Front cover art created by Steve Arnold by digital manipulation of *"LZ 127, Graf Zeppelin über dem Atlantik"*, originally illustrated by Theo Matejko, Germany, 1928

Back cover illustration by Steve Arnold

Printed in the United States of America

ISBN 979-8-9908505-0-7

FOR ANA,
WHO WAS THERE WHEN THE SKY FELL,
AND STAYED BEHIND TO PICK UP THE PIECES.

Acknowledgments

Thanks to everyone who helped in the creation of this book: Mike Eging for getting me hooked on writing as an avocation in the first place, and the invaluable input of Shane Portman and J. Drew Brumbaugh.

I

RAIN THRASHED the empty street, falling in sheets from midnight clouds invisible to the eye except where the darkness was pushed back by the thin light of gas-fueled streetlamps. The lamps were a relic of a past age's modernization, brought almost as an afterthought to Moroskaya, this forgotten northwestern backwater of the former Russian Empire, by Czar Nicholas just before the Great War. In those days they had been a symbol of *Progress* and *Prosperity* and had stood proudly between baroque shops whose hipped roofs nudged each other like dancers in a stage line.

Now, though, they were only morose sentinels of the night. Now the land bore the too-grand title of *The Moroskayan Soviet Socialist Republic* and was overseen by drably-uniformed commissars from the block-like government buildings at the end of the pavement that were lit, almost as a contrasting metaphor, by much starker electric lights.

Beyond these conflicting illuminations, the land rose in rolling slopes to another glow. This was a warmer light, faint but inviting, flickering behind rows of windows across the front of a large manor draped over the hills. This structure had spent its younger days as a hunting lodge for those same czars who had sought to bring some sophistication to the locals, and had about it a rustic air that was different from the elaborate architecture of the town or the squat resoluteness of the government buildings. The light within was small and moved from one glass pane to another in a deliberate arc.

The old butler Josef clutched the stair rail and pulled himself up, step by step, careful to keep the candle steady to light his way. He ignored the rain pounding against the windows on his left, just as he neglected the old poster adorning the wall to his right. It was a gaudy thing, to be sure, a playbill for a theater act of years gone by. The bold letters proclaimed the performance of Costan Campalia, "Sublime Master of Escape!" and depicted a mature man with silvered temples and a light-hearted expression, draped in chains and padlocks.

As the light of Josef's lamp drew away from the poster it shone in turn upon a series of photos, all showing various versions of Costan with his arms around a handsome woman, a young girl, and a younger boy. Everyone was smiling and the backgrounds were a travel catalogue all by themselves.

But in the last image, the children were older, the smiles were forced . . . and the woman was missing.

Josef moved on, hurrying as fast as his aching knees would safely take him. There was no time to waste.

A few paces beyond the head of the stairs he laid a veined hand upon the latch of a door and pushed it open without bothering to knock. A wedge of candlelight reached into the room and illuminated a cast-off pair of socks, a pile of adventure books, and a dusty easel supporting a long-unfinished landscape of the town below. He navigated the obstacles with care, stopping reflexively to replace a small fallen chess trophy on a shelf with others of its kind, on his way toward the bed where a young man lay sprawled half out of his covers.

Josef cleared his throat loudly. "Master Nilo, sir?" He took the three steps to the side of the bed and shook a protruding foot.

Nilo Campalia, the fourteen-year-old version of the boy in the photos, mumbled into his pillow and rolled away.

"Master Nilo!" Josef pressed, and shook the foot again. "Sir, you must wake up!"

Nilo grogged something through smacking lips and rose into a slumped but more-or-less upright posture.

"*What*, Josef? Is it morning already?" He plucked at his skewed pajamas to get them into some semblance of fit, scratched his head, and squinted at the thrumming windows.

"No, sir. It is just past midnight—"

Nilo made to fall back to his pillow but Josef clutched his shoulder and leaned close.

"There is a telephone call for you, sir! In the study!"

The old man's voice carried an intensity that finally seemed to reach through the fog in Nilo's dream-riddled head. "Midnight? . . . A call? A call . . . for *me*?"

"It's your father, sir. Master Costan—he is in the hospital. In Morograd!"

Nilo was suddenly wide awake. "Hospital! In Morograd? Wait—*Morograd?* Why? He's not supposed to play there for two weeks!"

In an instant the young man was belting on his robe and making for the stairs.

Within the study leather and dark-stained wood absorbed the light cast by the fireplace. The door swung open and Nilo crossed quickly to the desk, where he snatched up the hefty black phenolic telephone receiver.

"Hello?" The young man's voice only trembled slightly. "This is Nilo Campalia . . . yes, Costan Campalia's son. What happened to my father?"

Josef shuffled in behind and eased the door closed, face creased even more than usual with worry.

The voice on the other end of the phone was urgent and brief, and Nilo's brow knitted in concern. "'Catatonic'? Wait . . . what do you mean, 'as far as you can tell'?"

The voice in the receiver took on a protesting tone and Nilo's lips curled down into a frown. "Oh. I see," he said, though his voice revealed he really didn't. "Regulations. Well, yes. Of course. I will be there as soon as I can." He banged the receiver down on the hook. "And when I get there," he wondered aloud, "what am I going to do about 'regulations'?"

Many miles away, in an office painted in beige and sage and adorned with metal-framed cabinets and stainless steel furniture, a doctor cradled his own phone. He rubbed his stubbled jaw and looked into the shadows beyond the light of his desk lamp.

"That was him? He sounded like a kid."

The shadows did not answer right away, and the doctor grumbled under his breath. "I thought this 'Conductor' was a grown man." He raised his voice to a normal tone again. "I don't like this."

A tall shade disengaged itself from the darker shadows in the corner and stepped into the circle of light. It took shape as a man, well dressed, neatly groomed, and athletically built, wearing a cat-with-a-canary smile.

"The boy is only a means to an end. But you can take comfort, doctor," the Well-Dressed Man soothed, "in knowing that your cooperation will ensure that your facility will remain the last private hospital in Moroskaya." He adjusted his cuffs with meticulous precision. "At least for now."

"For now?" The doctor snorted. "Have a care, sir. We have powerful friends. We're not like those *kulaks* jumping the border for Inar Province."

"A tide I intend to stem," the Well-Dressed Man affirmed as he snugged his tie. "And as for your friends . . ." Two more men cast from the same mold stepped into the light and assumed the wide-footed, clasped-hand stance that had been the stock-in-trade for government agents since the days of Byzantium. The Well-Dressed Man didn't even glance at them. "Are your friends powerful enough?"

He arched an eyebrow suggestively and turned toward the door at the far end of the room, pausing long enough to incline his head back to the doctor who was now sitting bolt upright with clenched fists and a twisted frown.

"Your facility, doctor, is useful, make no mistake." The Well-Dressed Man plucked a dark gutter-dent fedora from a counter and settled it over his brow. "But it is not irreplaceable. Good night."

Josef politely cleared his throat. "Is everything all right, sir?" Like Nilo just before, his voice betrayed something else than what it said. Clearly, nothing was right. "Perhaps I should call Miss Lilya?"

"Lilya? Are you serious?"

The butler's face looked like a junkyard puppy that had been slapped—a little hurt, but with an indignant edge that was just a bit removed from showing teeth.

Nilo was quick to recover. "You know she wouldn't leave her duties to help him. She's too 'busy'." His voice was at once resigned, and peevish.

He frowned again. "No, I'm going to have to see what's going on before I even *think* about talking to Lilya."

II

THE DAWNING SUN rose into a clear sky over a meadow punctuated by wandering cattle. The scene was idyllic, like something straight out of one of Stalin's motivational posters—all it lacked was a strong-armed *babushka* in a short-sleeved work dress, hair tied back under a kerchief, wielding a hay-rake with a bright and encouraging smile.

Except, of course, for the armored cars parked on every hillock.

The soldiers sitting in the open hatches appeared bored. They lounged about listlessly and generally looked as though they wished they were closer together, if only so they could jibe their comrades as soldiers are wont to do when people aren't shooting at them.

Then . . . there was a sound.

It was almost subliminal at first, a distant rumble like a storm beyond the horizon. There was a high-pitched whine buried in it, though, that seemed to carry straight into one's teeth. One by one it got the soldiers' attention and they shaded their eyes to look to the east, straining to pick out the source in the glare of the new day.

First there was a speck. Then it was a dot, then a smudge, and suddenly it was a fast-moving crimson blur that blasted overhead at staggering speed and left shock waves rippling across the grasses with a noise like the air itself had been ripped in two. To a man, the soldiers' faces were left open-mouthed as it flashed by. It was a plane, but did it *move!* Even bootleg footage of the fastest aircraft at the races in Cleveland looked nothing like this.

As if that wasn't exciting enough, there was another detail that was not lost on these men who had been hand-picked to guard the flight tests of the newest product of Soviet military aviation.

It had no propellers.

It was a moderate size for an aircraft, maybe as big as a Twin Beech, and like the ubiquitous transport was adorned with a barrel-shaped nacelle on each wing. But it was sleek and stylish as an Auburn Speedster, and under the white-outlined Soviet star on the nose, a symbol of a white lily superimposed on an atom was underscored proudly with the name *Forerunner.*

Lilya Campalia, pale hair pulled into a tight bun, flicked steel-gray eyes over her instruments. Though the shoulder boards of her tailored flight suit only bore the single stripe of a junior lieutenant she carried an air of cool professionalism which was only enhanced by the gold star of a Hero Of The Soviet Union pinned at her left shoulder.

Her eyes returned to the horizon beyond the rakishly sloped windscreen and she keyed her intercom.

"Armas! Time!"

"*Thirty-two point four seconds, Comrade Lieutenant,*" came the reply over her headphones.

Six feet behind her, in the rear cockpit, Losily Armas nudged his thick spectacles up his nose, wiped his sweating palms on his baggy coveralls, and scanned his own instruments. Not for the first time in the hundred hours he had spent here over the last four months did he curse the gunner's pintle bolted to his panel that always seemed to be in the way.

He covered his microphone with his hand and muttered under his breath, "This time for sure."

Meanwhile, Lilya was marking the rapidly decreasing distance to a lattice-work tower dead ahead. She flipped a switch on her radio panel and put her microphone to her lips again.

"Lieutenant Campalia to Control. Approaching outer marker. Surge Power on standby." Her brow creased for an instant and she switched back to the intercom. "Armas?"

Armas checked his panels once again and crossed his fingers. "Yes, Comrade Lieutenant. All lights are green."

Lilya nodded to herself. "Stand by." She snugged her harness down and forced herself to loosen her grip on the Forerunner's control stick. "Pylon in three—"

The *Forerunner* skimmed over a slender pillar painted in bright orange six hundred meters from the pylon.

Armas tightened his own seat belts, wiped the sweat off his hands again, and re-crossed his fingers.

"Two—"

A second pillar disappeared under the ship's nose. Four hundred meters.

"One—"

The third and final pillar was passed and the weblike tower filled the windscreen.

"*Mark!*"

Lilya slammed the twin throttles forward, flicked the metal stop tab out of the way and pushed the handles further. The whine from the engines grew louder and higher in pitch until it was almost beyond hearing. She hauled back on the control stick at the same time until only sky was visible before her, and the view of the ground in her rear-view mirror was rippled by the blast of blue-flamed thrust from the engines.

In the back Armas had no attention to spare for the incredible forces just a few arm-lengths away. His eyes were glued to his indicators that, to an engineer, told more of what was going on in the wings than mere eyesight could, and would react faster to any anomalies.

This was 'Surge Power'. Sure, the Germans had developed a turbine engine, and it had been months since Heinkel had flown them in their Model 178. There were even rumors the firm was putting together a fighter aircraft using the revolutionary 'jet' powerplants. But much to the Luftwaffe's disappointment the 178 hadn't been any faster than aircraft already in use and was hampered by a severely limited range.

The *Forerunner*, on the other hand, flew with something completely different—the so-called Nuclear Induction Motor operating on principles of splitting the very atoms of matter, first researched at Tavrida University in Kiev. It had incredible range on startlingly little fuel and when the power was 'surged' by as-yet highly classified means, could rival a rocket for sheer energy.

And right now she was blasting into the sky like a homesick meteor.

Lilya allowed the acceleration to push her back into the pilot's seat. Though she was tight-lipped her wide-eyed expression would have betrayed the thrill she was feeling to anyone who could have seen it.

Armas didn't, sitting in the back facing the rear, and in any case was too preoccupied with his concerns to allow such a cast to his own features.

"Surge Power at forty-five percent . . . fifty . . ." As the power indicators inched upward, so did the pitch of his voice. ". . . fifty-five, fifty-six, fifty-seven—"

In a heartbeat a swath of lights on the left side of his panel flashed red. The port engine let out a *bang!* and vibrations began thrashing the airframe.

Lilya cut the throttles, but it was too late. The *Forerunner* flipped inverted and began spiraling to the ground. In an instant the reassuring throb of the engines was gone, replaced by the unnervingly natural howl of air rushing over the canopy—not a sound any pilot wants to hear.

"*Nyet!* Armas!"

To make matters worse the balking engine was more than just dead weight on the left wing. Unlike the idling starboard motor which at least allowed air to pass through it, the left's large intake was acting just like a metal parachute, dragging the ship hard to the left and intensifying the flat spin Lilya was struggling to counter with all her might. And as if that wasn't enough, it was disrupting the airflow over the wing and shaking the craft like a dog with a shoe, making even simple tasks like flipping a switch nearly impossible.

Armas howled in terror as his spectacles threatened to slide off his face, anxiously throwing levers and cranking valves.

Lilya fought to once again bend the stricken craft to her will as spinning ground filled her vision. *"Armas!"*

At last, the engineer's efforts paid off. The angry indicator lights settled into a surly amber and the buffeting stopped as the engine spun back up to a tolerably smooth fast idle. Lilya was finally able to right the craft and with a final push on the stick broke out of the spin and pulled the *Forerunner*'s nose back up to the horizon.

Armas smoothed his tousled hair back with a shaking hand as the grasslands, flogged by the *Forerunner*'s wake, slid by only a few dozen feet below. He spared a disgusted glance to the portside engine, now trailing sickly vapors to the tune of a spitting grumble.

Lilya limped the *Forerunner* into a slow climb and keyed the intercom. "Number One converter again! I thought you had addressed that?"

Armas loosened his harness and swallowed hard. He forced a smile. "An engineer walks into a shop and says, 'You don't have any converters, do you, Comrade?'"

"Armas . . ." Lilya warned.

"The shop man says, 'You are mistaken, Comrade Engineer. This is the paint shop. We have no paint—'"

"Armas . . ."

"'The parts department is in the next block. *They* don't have any converters!'"

"Armas!"

Armas' mouth curled down into a chagrined frown. "My apologies, Comrade Lieutenant. I will repair it. Have no fear."

Lilya shook her head without sympathy. "*You* have no fear. May Day is coming and the Fritzes will be there. Nobody knows how long this truce with Hitler is going to last and they need to be shown where they stand." Now it was her turn to wipe the sweat from her palms. "I'm calling Control. This day is done."

"But our testing protocol—" Armas twisted around until he could just see Lilya's face in the rear-view mirror. "Um. Yes, Comrade Lieutenant. A wise decision."

On the ground the guardsmen, still open-mouthed, watched the *Forerunner* waddle into the sunrise, trailing steam.

III

THE *NORTHERN EXPRESS* swept past farms, breezed around villages, and coursed through factory complexes on its impatient route into Morograd.

Within the dining car, Nilo played chess with a fellow passenger. "Checkmate," the old man declared, almost apologetically. "You feeling all right, son?"

"I shouldn't have gone with the English opening." Nilo shrugged. "Outstanding game, sir . . . . I'm all right. Just got a lot on my mind."

"Don't feel bad, son." The old man smiled. "The English is a good opening. But—" he waved a hand over the board, "one shouldn't play if you can't watch all the pieces. That's a recipe for disaster!"

"Sound advice, sir. I will keep it in mind."

There was a slight lurch as the train began to slow. Nilo stood, donned his coat, and offered the man a handshake. "This is my stop. Thanks for the game . . . and the advice."

The old man cackled sarcastically. "Take my advice, son. I'm not using it!" He guffawed at his joke and winked at Nilo as he boxed up the board. "You be careful out there, my lad."

"I will, sir. You as well."

He made his way to the car's vestibule as the Express slowed to a halt in the Moroskaya Station, venting steam in shrill billows. Once the conductor unhooked the chain across the ladder he stepped down onto the platform and looked around.

Steel and concrete arced overhead in dizzying vaults. Panes of iron-framed glass admitted bright sunlight like some giant insect that was, for a change, watching the humans below. Self-important men and women in suits and overcoats jostled workmen in coveralls and boots, all pushing past Nilo intent on their many personal missions. On an adjacent track, a row of dull-colored cars swarmed with young soldiers in ill-fitting uniforms, massive packs on their backs, who were giving their loved ones last kisses and hugs before boarding under the hoarse directions of their sergeants.

As he turned toward the exits there was a sudden, blinding flash, a palpable concussion, and then everything went black.

It seemed like a very long time before he came to his senses, but Nilo could tell it was only seconds. Shards of glass were still raining from the ceiling and everything still sounded like it was a long way off in a tunnel.

Smoke was everywhere. Boots were running past him toward the troop train where the engine burned fiercely. Even allowing for his dulled hearing Nilo noticed the air was eerily silent—for about three heartbeats.

Then the screams began, as the injured realized they were hurt, and fear set in.

Voices with authoritative timbres rose above the din and began directing laying of fire hoses and movement of bystanders. Nilo was helped roughly to his feet, pushed along in the direction of what he hoped were the exits, and then found himself left to his own devices. He staggered aimlessly for a moment and wondered about his baggage until a man in a rail service uniform laid a hand on his shoulder and guided him out of the way of incoming police officers. He found a curb alongside the wall out of the way and sat down to wait for the chaos to sort itself out.

Within an hour the fire was under control and the most severely wounded had been transported away. Everyone else, on the other hand, had been rounded up and were standing in nervous ranks on the platform as grim-faced constables ranged up and down their lines, asking questions and generally being skeptical of the answers.

Nilo was checking his watch and trying to recall when visiting hours would be over when a shadow fell over him. He looked up into the narrow gaze of a veteran officer behind an impressive mustache that looked as though it had three confirmed arrests of its own.

The man held out a hand. "Papers," he demanded tiredly, until his eye caught on a pin on Nilo's lapel. The ornament was rather large and sported a winged propeller surmounted by a red star. "Comrade Stalin's *Komsomol* aside," he challenged, "aren't you a little young for an Air Force Excellency badge?"

"Um? Oh . . . it's my sister's."

The officer's cocked eyebrow spoke volumes.

"You've probably heard of her," Nilo explained, suddenly feeling like everyone around him had taken a step back. "Lilya Campalia?"

The man's facial hair curled up into a sneer to match the eyebrow. "Oh, indeed? Your sister is the famous Night Witch of the Winter War?" Though that conflict against the Finns had not gone well for the Soviet State in a political sense, it had given the military invaluable experience and had produced a handful of unlikely heroes.

He took Nilo's wallet and glanced at it, then did a double-take. "Hmpf."

Nilo smiled blandly as the officer slowly traced his thumb along the entries on the document.

"Then your papa would be that Houdini character, Costan the Great, or some such?"

"'The Sublime Costan'." Nilo nodded but he felt it would be a good idea to get the subject of this conversation off his family. He rubbernecked past the officer's shoulder. "So this—" He cocked his chin at the remnants of the smoldering train. "Rebels from Inar?"

The older man barely spared a glance at the damage. "Ungrateful bastards. We should have left them to the Swedes years ago."

"Why do they do it, you think?"

"Why do *you* think? The Secretary-General cleans house, heads roll, and their favorite rabble-rousers wind up in Lubyanka Prison. They suddenly come to realize they have to do what they're told . . . can make one a bit testy."

"Testy. Yeah . . ." Nilo swept his eyes over the wreckage. "You see a lot of this here?"

The officer's gaze narrowed again and Nilo once again had the feeling of being alone in a very crowded room. "Papa's in the hospital," he offered.

"Is he, now? And why is that?"

"I don't know." Nilo put an edge in his voice he really didn't feel. "I only heard . . . something suddenly unfortunate had happened to him." He looked pointedly at the devastated locomotive, then back to the officer.

The constable eyed Nilo for a long moment and he forced himself not to squirm. Nothing good comes from showing the predator your fear, he thought to himself.

Eventually the constable snorted, slapped Nilo's wallet shut and thrust it back to him. "You just be sure, little bunny," he said with a look that offered no such endearment, "to check in at the hospital when you get there."

The Well-Dressed Man stood at the knee wall surrounding the roof of the Morograd Hospital and watched an automobile cab dodge errant pedestrians and horse-carts to screech to a halt at the main entrance. The door opened and a young man in an overcoat that looked as though it had been rolled over a construction site got out, paid the cabbie, and stepped up to the soldier guarding the entrance. He offered his papers and was admitted within.

The man turned to the impassive agent at his elbow. "You can close down the city now. No civilian traffic in or out."

The agent nodded. "He will do what we need, sir?"

"The doctor will see to it. He doesn't dare risk his position."

"What if the boy can't convince her?"

"Not to worry. I have a fallback." The Well-Dressed Man pushed back off the parapet, dusted the side of his shoe, and turned for the stairwell.

The nurse was a pretty brunette with the wide cheekbones of the *Rus* and the harried pale blue eyes of the chronically overworked. She opened the hospital room door and stepped aside as the doctor ushered Nilo in.

Nilo took two quick steps over the threshold and pulled up short.

On the far side of the room, slumped in a chair by the window, was his father Costan. Not the vibrant and cocksure man he knew, but a disheveled shell that stared beyond the trees and haltingly muttered a single word over and over again.

"... *Boyan* ... *Boyan* ... *Boyan* ..."

Nilo looked back at the doctor, then to Costan, then to the doctor again.

"Since he was brought in last night," the doctor explained.

Nilo looked for something in the doctor's expression, some illumination, but found none. He turned to the nurse, anxiously drumming her fingers on the side of her jaw, whose preoccupied mien at least offered a sympathetic arc to her brow as she inched along the open door to the hall. "Will there be anything else, sir?"

The doctor shook his head absently and leaned a hip against the sink. "No, Tatanya, that's all we need, thank you."

She exited quickly and closed the door, sealing out the noise in the hall and settling a blanket of oppressive silence over the room.

Nilo shook himself and took a breath. "How did he get here?"

"Someone dropped him off and left."

Nilo tread slowly up to Costan's chair, knelt beside it and took his father's unresistant hand.

"Papa? Papa, can you hear me?"

"... *Boyan* ..." Costan stared blankly out the window. After a moment Nilo let go his hand, but the limb remained extended until Nilo gently pushed it back down to the armrest. He spoke over his shoulder to the doctor. "Have you given him anything? Medications, I mean?"

"No. He hasn't been agitated or combative. To be truthful I'm not sure exactly what's really wrong with him."

Nilo studied his father. He wasn't sure what he was looking for, but a nagging fear was creeping into his heart that they wouldn't be going home that night. "Papa? It's Nilo ... Papa?"

"That's not going to work."

"How long will you be keeping him?"

"Actually," the doctor crossed his arms, "we won't be."

"I'm sorry?"

"Our psychiatric ward doesn't have a bed to spare. We had to fill all the beds ... the train, you know."

"Oh . . . I see." Worries raced through his head as he tried to figure out his next step. He hadn't planned on this, though in reality he wasn't sure what he *had* planned on.

He needed time. "Can you keep him one more night? We can cover the bill."

"Oh, don't worry about that. The bill's been taken care of."

"It has? By whom?"

The doctor stood upright and placed a hand on the door handle. "In my work I've found it's sometimes better just to take the money." He opened the door and nodded suggestively.

Nilo sighed and got to his feet.

"All right, then." He laid his coat over his arm. "I guess I'll be back."

At the ward desk, Nurse Tatanya jotted notes in a chart and tried to ignore the Well-Dressed Man and his companion lounging by her elbow.

Nilo exited his father's room ahead of the doctor and walked past her station as if the weight of the world was on his shoulders, but Tatanya noticed his look out the side of his eye toward the two men encroaching on her space.

For her own part she made what she felt was a valiant attempt to not watch the Well-Dressed Man as he marked the passage of the boy. She forced her eyes in the opposite direction, which just happened to be straight to the other agent. She was startled to see *he* was watching *her*.

The agent raised his brow, but his eyelids remained slitted.

She knew instantly what he wanted. "As soon as he returns, sir," she confirmed.

The agent gave her a small nod and touched the Well-Dressed Man's shoulder.

She continued to try not to watch them as they left.

IV

L ATER THAT NIGHT Nilo was back in the room, sitting in front of Costan with a folding table between them bearing what was left of their dinner.

At least, Nilo's, as Costan's plate was untouched.

Nilo lifted a cup to him. "Tea, Papa? How about a tart?"

When Costan made no move to respond Nilo set the cup back down and sagged. "How did this happen to you?"

"...*Boyan*..."

"Boyan." Nilo snorted in frustration. "Who is Boyan?"

"...*Boyan*..."

"Boyan is Boyan. That's helpful." Nilo got up and paced the room. It was sparsely furnished, which was no surprise, but in a drawer in the vanity he found his father's personal effects—a cap and scarf to ward off the damp air, a pair of gloves, and...

Nilo reached in and withdrew a large leather wallet. He laid it on the counter with obvious reverence and gently unfolded one side.

Within was a collection of small tools. They had the look of dental implements, with plain polished handles and odd-shaped twists and serrations on their business ends.

Lockpicks. An idea slid into Nilo's mind like a mischievous worm but he ignored it for the moment.

He laid open the other fold of the wallet to reveal a creased sheet of thick paper. Curious, he picked it up and spread it out. It was one of his father's old handbills, and Nilo felt a pang of loss when he looked at the photo of the dynamic performer and compared it to what sat before him.

It was then that he noticed something had dropped out of the folded bill. Two things, actually.

One was a pale gray corner of a newspaper page, fairly new by the look of it.

The other was a pressed lily, white, flat, and brittle.

He frowned at the lily and set it carefully aside, turning his attention to the shred of paper. There was writing on it and he was startled to see it was his father's hand, with an urgent scrawl to it.

Lilya— Nilo—

Help me!

Nilo quickly scrutinized the inked printing. "Yesterday's date," he mused aloud, and looked at his father once more. Apprehension was again building in his stomach, but this was a different kind than what he had felt earlier that afternoon.

"What kind of game is—"

There was a respectful knock at the door. It nudged open and Tatanya peeked into the room. "Sir? Visiting hours are over for the night."

"Oh!" Nilo crumpled the newsprint up in his hand and slipped it behind him. "Yes, right. I'll just see myself out, thanks."

Tatanya nodded and left, leaving the door open as a reminder that his time was up. Nilo carefully folded the pressed lily into the handbill and slipped it back into the wallet, his jaw set.

"So it's an *Italian* opening, then, is it?"

He thrust the wallet into his coat pocket, reopened the note, and studied it more closely, but no more insights were forthcoming.

He tapped the note and frowned. "Fine, then," he said to himself. "Pawn to King Four."

A short while later Nilo was nodding briefly at the soldier standing at the hospital's main entrance as he stepped past him into the street. It had been drizzling while he had been trying to dine with his father, and the air smelled earthy over the shimmering reflections of the streetlights.

Across the way he noticed the Well-Dressed Man that had been hanging around the ward slide into the passenger seat of a black sedan that immediately took off with a tinny roar.

Nilo looked both ways, then flagged the soldier's attention again. "Place to eat?"

The young trooper waved to the left. "Most places are toward the center of town."

Nilo stared down the avenue in that direction. "Thanks!"

"But it's a hike, brother."

"That's all right," Nilo reassured him, and set off at a quick pace.

Once he was most of a block away and beyond the immediate lights, though, he slipped into an alley and circled back to the deep shadows along the flank of the hospital, where he found a lonely service door under a small floodlamp.

He pulled out the lockpicks and set to work. It was only a moment until the door popped open with a *snick*.

"Most dads teach their kids how to fish," Nilo muttered as he darted inside out of sight.

The file room was pitch black, sequestered as it was in the basement on the alley side of the building. Only the subdued thrum of the heating ducts watched over the ranked file cabinets.

Which was fortunate for Nilo as he released another door latch under the dim illumination of the widely-spaced bulbs in the outer corridor and finally attained his objective.

Now to complete the mission.

He padded quickly down the main aisle scanning labels with a small flashlight. A turn here, a reach there, then a stoop to the bottom drawer . . . his fingers rifled through manila folders and stopped.

"And who's playing White?" he whispered to himself.

He yanked up the file, flipped it open, and strained to read it in the dim light of his hand lamp. A quick scan down the page and he had it.

Though he was stumped as to what to do with it. He read it again, out loud just to be sure.

"Diagnosis 'Catatonia'. Cash receipt to . . . Jedric Orianos?"

He closed the file, shut the drawer, and leaned against the cabinet in the dark.

"Really? *Jedric Orianos?*"

Clouds billowed serenely over the chill sparkling waters of the Gulf of Inar. To the west lay the rugged shores of Scandinavia against the North Sea; to the east rose the rolling farmlands of Moroskaya's Inar Province, gateway to the Soviet Union's northwestern verge.

And hotbed of civil unrest.

Above this, among those clouds like an artificial analogue, cruised the *Spirit Walker*. It was a rigid-framed airship as white and nearly as large as the cumulonimbi with which it kept company. It was built along the lines of the infamous zeppelins of the Kaiser's *Deutsche Luftstreitkräfte* of the War, but much unlike its more aggressive progenitors no weapons marred its lines—it was beautifully symmetric except for the expansive flat deck built into its upper surface.

This was the singular feature that really set the *Spirit Walker* apart, for it was over that surface that garishly-painted private aircraft of the influential and the well-heeled orbited, waiting their turn with uncharacteristic patience to land and disembark their passengers for a unique experience with one of the most renowned clairvoyants of the Age.

The dinner theater on the middle deck was tastefully paneled in lightweight mahogany. It was a detail invisible in the darkened chamber, but the elegantly-dressed patrons present would not have cared anyway, as their attention was riveted on the stage.

A man stood there, alone, in a white dinner jacket highlighted by a crimson lapel flower. His youthful face was clean-shaven, and framed eyes carrying a wisdom beyond his years. At this moment they were focused beyond the boa-bedecked matron that stood beside her table directly before him, whose own eyes were wide, and a touch apprehensive.

The man on the stage was reaching out, elbow locked, wrist extended, fingers spread like he was clutching at life itself—which to his benefactors he actually seemed to be doing. Hovering in the air between him and the woman was a misty, man-sized form. It swirled, rotated, seemed to collect itself . . . and gradually dissipated into mist.

The woman swooned into the arms of her startled tablemates. The man on the stage slumped, panting heavily, and dabbed at the sweat on his brow with a kerchief from his sleeve. He then looked back up with an apologetic smile, and the audience erupted in applause.

The Master of Ceremonies dashed onstage with a chair to place under the man as he sagged, and raised a hand for the peoples' attention.

"Jedric Orianos, ladies and gentlemen!"

The lights came up and stagehands stepped in to help Jedric off the stage as the Master of Ceremonies tried to carry on his announcements through the din.

"We hope you enjoyed this demonstration, friends. Rest assured Mr. Orianos will be available for questions later this evening. For now, though, please enjoy your meal."

Backstage Jedric politely shrugged off the stagehands with a smile and toweled his face.

A stately middle-aged woman in a Merchant Marine Commander's uniform approached him. "Sir!"

"Ursula." Even Jedric's voice was as courtly as a marble pillar. He leaned in close. "What's our status?"

"Our last delivery will arrive within twelve hours."

"Good. Did you get rid of the Colonel?"

"Already disembarked, sir." She caught the next question in Jedric's upraised brow. "He seemed satisfied with what we gave him."

"Outstanding work, as always, Ursula. Meet me on the bridge in ten."

V

NILO FACED the dour airfield guards and stood his ground. "Sorry, kid," the sergeant was huffing over his morning hot tea ration. "No one said anything to us about you."

Not far off a gaggle of youthful onlookers were crowding the fence, trying to get a glimpse into the door of the hangar a hundred yards away where the *Forerunner* was parked and her pilot, the skilled and beautiful Lieutenant Campalia, was sure any moment to appear.

The hangar doors began to roll open and the crowd of fans became excited. A few started leaping up the chain linking in their exuberance.

The sergeant took two steps away from the gate toward them. "You there!" he bellowed in a voice that would have chilled the blood of a recruit, "Step back! *I said STEP BACK!*"

Nilo took the advantage and sprinted past him for the hangar.

"Hey!" the sergeant growled, then waved angrily at his corporal. "Keep these in line while I get that one!"

Inside the hangar civilian workers in coveralls emblazoned with the logo of the Apostolov Design Bureau orbited the *Forerunner* and shook their heads at the work laid before them . . . again.

Nilo pushed the last few yards into the building but pulled up short as he nearly collided with Lilya coming around the far side of the aircraft. The huffing sergeant grabbed Nilo by the shoulder. "Got you!"

Lilya's face was impassive as she stared Nilo down. "Little brother."

The sergeant hesitated. At a worktable a few feet away Armas looked up, waved familiarly to Nilo, but turned quickly back to his task when he caught sight of Lilya's face.

She glanced at the guard, her eyes annoyed, though not at him. "I have it from here, sergeant."

"Ma'am!" The soldier released Nilo, snapped Lilya a brisk salute, and stomped off to the gate.

Lilya regarded Nilo with a critical eye. "Nilo. I received your telegram. What's with Father?"

Nilo watched the sergeant march away. He was sure he could hear the man muttering under his breath even from here. "Thanks for that, Lilya, I—"

"Nilo!" Her admonition cut him off mid-stream. "Father? You said he was catatonic?"

"Um . . ." Nilo fumbled. Things had been tense between him and his sister for the last two years, but he had thought, surely now, with this . . . . "I guess. The doctor didn't seem exactly certain."

"He didn't? Did he *seem* to have any idea when he *would* be certain?" Her voice was beginning to take on a hint of disdain.

"Well . . . no."

"No?" It wasn't a question so much as it was a critique. "What is this doctor's plan for him? He does have a plan?"

"Well, Lilya . . . that's the problem."

Lilya rocked back on one heel and folded her arms. "I'm not following you."

"Lilya, I need—I need you to sign him out."

Her brow arched in surprise. "You need me to what?"

The look in her eyes was more than he could bear, and the words started spilling out of Nilo's mouth. "The doctor isn't sure what's wrong. He isn't sure what he can do, or when he'll get better. Or even . . . or even *if* he'll get better, and they don't have the room to keep him, so he has to go, and I thought . . ."

"You will be taking him home, yes?"

Nilo stopped and said nothing, not being sure at this point what the right thing to say would be.

Lilya put her hands on her hips and leaned forward. "You weren't expecting *me* to?"

"I . . . was?"

It was Lilya's turn to remain silent, though likely for entirely different reasons.

Nilo shuffled his feet and stuck his hands in his pockets. "Look, Lilya, I don't know how to do these things, I'm not old enough to sign for nurses, supplies, medical bills—"

"Josef can do it. He does it all the time when Father's on the road."

"But that's because he could get Papa a telegram, or phone him when there was a question! There's going to be questions! Decisions to be made! I mean, does his will go into effect when something like this happens?" Nilo's voice took on a desperate edge. "I thought—"

"I don't have room for him."

"But Lilya—"

"Or the time."

"Lilya!"

"Nilo Costanovich. End of discussion." If the words themselves weren't enough of an indication she was through, her tone certainly was. She turned away to take a clipboard and pen from the Apostolov foreman.

"But Lilya, I don't know what we're going to do with him!"

Lilya stopped, closed her eyes, sighed, and handed the clipboard back. "Nilo. Calm yourself. This isn't like you. Is he really that bad?"

"He is. He just sits there."

"He does nothing at all?"

"Are you even listening?"

"Don't take that surly tone with me. Has he said anything?"

"He kept mumbling a name . . . Boyan?"

"Boyan? Who is Boyan?"

"Search me. I was hoping you knew."

"Not by half. You know I don't speak to him." She waved the foreman away with a come-back-in-a-few-minutes expression and folded her arms again. "How did he even get there?"

"*That's* the weird part. Would you believe he was left there by—" Nilo took a breath for dramatic effect, "Jedric Orianos?"

Lilya stifled a laugh. "Jedric Orianos? The famous medium? He was there?"

"Not that I know of. But his name was on the bill."

"But who is he to Father?" Her eyes narrowed. "And how did you know his name was on the bill?"

Nilo's tone became sheepish. "Because I broke into the file room to look."

Lilya shook her head and her eyes darkened. "Little brother. You're turning into a troublemaker. Keep that up and you'll end up like Father."

"What's that supposed to mean?"

"Bending the rules. Roving the world for applause." She turned back to the foreman and waved for the clipboard again, which she signed with an impatient hand. "Forgetting your own family."

"Lilya, don't."

"Why not?" She turned back to Nilo and her eyes were smoldering. "Has *he* paid us any mind since Mama died? Any at all?"

"She was his best friend!"

"And we were his children!"

"You still wear Mama's ring!"

Lilya snapped her arms folded again to hide the elegant silver band on her finger.

Nilo pressed on. "You miss her still. So does Papa."

"But he doesn't miss us."

"That's enough, Lilya."

"He *forgot* us, Nilo."

"*That's enough, Lilya!*"

They stepped apart, facing away from each other, and tried to ignore the soldiers and technicians that were trying to ignore them.

After a long and awkward moment, Lilya took a deep breath. "I am sorry, Nilo." She breathed deeply again as if to wash out the anger from her voice. "It was just too hard."

When Nilo spoke, his voice was small and vulnerable. "Will you come to the hospital?" He turned back to his sister and his expression was imploring. "Please?"

Lilya turned back to him, and beyond him saw Armas focusing too hard on his work.

She blew out her breath, shrugged out of her flight suit, and grabbed a well-adorned leather jacket.

"Armas."

The engineer fumbled the wrench in his hand. "Ma'am?"

"I will be going to the hospital now."

"Yes, Comrade Lieutenant."

Nilo relaxed, at least a bit. Now for the pawn break, he thought. "I have a cab waiting," he said in a helpful tone.

Lilya wrinkled her nose. "We'll take my car."

VI

NILO HURRIED to keep up with Lilya. "You parked far enough away," he groused. It wasn't just the distance that bothered him. Unlike this morning when he had crossed mostly empty streets to the airfield, now they were pushing through a thick mass of people on the sidewalks and he really just didn't like crowds.

As they reached the main avenue he finally saw why.

The route had been cleared of all traffic and the center of the street was taken up by marching troops. They were goose-stepping smartly along in dress uniforms, swinging their arms like clockwork mannequins, and looking to the far side of the way where a red-bunted platform supported a round-faced man orating loudly with a shaking fist.

Some of the thronging bystanders waved tiny red flags eagerly, others did so with less fervor. The animated flag-wavers glowered at the less ardent.

"At least that explains where we parked," Nilo observed. He looked at Lilya with a question in his eyes.

"Every day since Inar broke away," she answered.

As if especially to add emphasis to her statement, at that moment a bottle arced overhead trailing a wick of fire to shatter on the pavement.

Flames splattered and the parade erupted into pandemonium. There was a ragged chorus of shouts of *Za Inarya!* and *Smert Stalinu!* from somewhere behind them and more bottles and rocks flew. Little red flags were flung away as the crowds bolted for cover. Black-clad figures with faces masked by blue scarves darted into the panicking masses, swinging clubs and fists as the soldiers clustered into defensive groups and looked anxiously to their officers.

"Inar rebels!" Lilya yelled to Nilo. "Here, in here!" She dragged him down an alley and pushed him on ahead of her so they wouldn't be trampled.

They ran for what felt like a long time. It seemed they dodged in and out of streets and alleys with abandon, though Nilo was dimly aware of Lilya shouting directions and he blindly obeying. After some minutes they stopped, gasping for air behind a grimy restaurant.

The sound of rioting was fainter, but only just, and only for a moment. Lilya cocked an ear carefully.

"They're getting closer." She looked down at herself. "It's my uniform. It's drawing too much attention. Here," she said, whipping off her cap, "put this in your coat."

Nilo shoved it into an inside pocket as she pulled off her jacket and tied it inside-out around her waist, then took his hand and led him onward.

At the head of the next alley, she paused and looked both ways. The street was clear, but as she stepped out shots echoed from a plaza a dozen yards to their left. A stampede of rioters spilled around the corner, heading their way.

"*Jó mojó*!" Lilya fumed. She pulled Nilo into a tenement building and smoothly pushed call buttons until an unwitting resident buzzed the foyer door. She snapped it open, yanked Nilo in, and ducked him panting into the stairwell as the rampage passed them by.

Once again Tatanya opened the hospital room door. Nilo stepped doggedly in, but Lilya halted on the threshold.

Unbidden, a memory arose in her mind, grabbing her attention like a dog with a new carcass . . .

Her father Costan is chained in an elaborate trap on a spotlit stage before a thrilled audience. Dramatic music is playing somewhere, heightening the tension. Her mother Ilse, always elegant, holds the final lock.

That's her cue. Lilya's moment on the stage.

She scampers out into the light, her eleven-year-old crown decked in white flowers. She reaches her father and snaps the lock closed as she sings:

> *"A lock you cannot break,*
>
> *A chain you cannot shake,*
>
> *The trap 'compassing your heart . . ."*

Little Nilo, barely five, follows her out and makes a show of trying to pick the lock until Ilse scoops him up and carries him away. Lilya plucks one of the flowers from her tiara and places it in Costan's ear, kisses him sweetly, and scampers offstage waving endearingly to vigorous applause . . .

"Well," was all she could manage.

"You see what I mean," Nilo whispered.

Lilya walked slowly to her father, knelt and eyed him critically. *This* had once been the man that had been her hero. *This* had been the world to her, until that night two years ago. Even afterward he had loomed on the backdrop of her life, strong, resolute, clever, and resourceful. She had felt he was undeniably capable of literally *anything* he would put his mind to. Truly an intimidating shadow to crawl out from.

But then what in the world . . . was *this*?

Nilo approached from the other side and touched Costan's shoulder.

"Papa? Lilya's here."

There was no answer, not even the mysterious mantra 'Boyan', only the blank stare out the window.

"Papa?" Nilo coaxed.

"Spare yourself, Nilo." Lilya's voice was sober.

"I just don't understand how this could have happened."

Lilya stood and exhaled loudly. "It's just the next step in a journey he started a long time ago." She turned away and nodded to the nurse. "Let me just get this dealt with."

The crowds had been disbursed, though the pavements were still littered with glass and debris and now soldiers were posted at every corner.

Lilya eased down the street in her car. Despite her wishes to finish this task with as little ado as possible the machine managed to draw the envious stares of every single one of the boys in green. Small wonder, being as it was a ZiS 101 Sport, a sleek machine with an in-line eight-cylinder engine and a low-slung, aggressive stance. Only a few had been built and the fact she had one issued to her was as clear an indication to the rank-and-file as anything of her celebrity status.

The downside was that, though it was built on a limousine frame it was only a two-placer and Costan was sagging in the passenger seat. This left Nilo curled up uncomfortably in the cramped space to the rear that was supposed to be only for small bags and stowing the folding top.

He shifted to relieve the pressure on his buttocks and toyed with the scrap of newspaper.

"They've grounded civilian air traffic. Because of the train and all."

"Yes." Lilya checked a crossing street, eased out the clutch, and turned south for the airfield. "Is that important?"

Nilo yelped when the car hit a hole in the road.

"Nilo?"

He hesitated. He knew what he needed to say, but he also knew Lilya would shut him down before he could even explain himself—

"Nilo? I said—"

"We need to see Jedric."

"What?"

Nilo hesitated again and cursed his weakness in the face of Lilya's response. "We need to see—"

"I know what you said," Lilya snapped. She pulled out onto the airfield circuit road and smoothly shifted into high gear. "What I don't get is why you said it. Why do we need to see Jedric?"

"He paid the bill. He has to know what happened." He sulked lower in his tiny niche. "He could help."

"Why do you think he would help?" Her tone was that of a teacher to a lackluster student.

"He has to!" Nilo blurted.

"Does he? Why? This isn't one of your novels, Nilo."

"But he was the last person to see Papa . . . normal."

Lilya shook her head. "Now that's the part I don't understand. What was he doing with Father? He was never into that spiritualism garbage."

"So?"

"So what would he have been doing with the likes of Jedric Orianos?" She pulled up to the airfield gate, flashed her identification card at the guard, and passed within. "I say we let the doctor sort it out."

"But he said he couldn't unless he knew how Papa got this way!"

"I think we are just seeing the next rung on a ladder he started down after Mama died."

"Don't say that. Just don't."

"Why not?" Lilya pulled off the drive and braked to a halt. She twisted around to look at Nilo, brows drawn together. "What are you looking for, Nilo? A culprit? Someone you can *make* fix him?" She waved a hand impatiently at Costan. "What if he did it to himself?"

"No, Lilya! Someone did this to him!"

"Oh? Found a confession, did you?"

Nilo's eyes grew dark and he glared at the newsprint in his hand, then shoved it into his pocket.

Lilya shook her head and put the car back into gear.

In the hangar office, Armas swallowed hard and looked up into the impassive eyes of the agent. The bigger man had clamped the engineer's shoulders like a vice and was lifting him onto his tiptoes.

Behind him the Well-Dressed Man leaned in close and spoke softly into his ear, though his words carried all the compassion of a blackjack across the face.

"I have full confidence you will give it your best effort. Just make sure she listens to her brother."

The agent released Armas with a shove and wiped his hands. The Well-Dressed Man clapped Armas companionably on the shoulder as he came around, making Armas jump, and touched his finger to the brim of his hat in a mocking salute as they exited out a side door.

Armas could only stare after them, eyes wide with fear.

Lilya pulled the car into the hangar and shut it down, then climbed out and crossed to her locker without looking back. Nilo half-fell out the door after her and circled around to get Costan out.

Lilya reached into her locker and exchanged her jacket for her coverall. "Remember, Nilo, Jedric lives on that airship of his. He doesn't come down here. His patrons fly up to him."

"Right," Nilo admitted, trying to get Costan steady on his feet. "And you have a plane."

"I do *not* have a plane. The *Forerunner* is a remarkable accomplishment of the people and it belongs to them."

"But you're the pilot. You're famous! You could—" He paused to carefully release Costan, who now stood, stooped and lost, by the car. "Lilya, we have to do *something.*"

"Yes," she said decisively as she zipped up her flight suit. "I will hire a nurse and you will take him home."

She stepped away to the workbench and started thumbing through the *Forerunner's* testing schedule. "Goodness knows I don't want to."

Armas watched them from the office door, then slowly turned and looked to the side door the Well-Dressed Man had departed through only a short time before. Armas breathed deep, squared his shoulders, and caught the chief technician looking at him.

"Today's lesson, boys and girls," he said, "is on 'Poking The Bear'."

The chief technician's expression was baffled.

Armas' expression softened and his tone became more paternal. "Take five, Grekov . . . and your lads."

As the crew cleared the hangar Armas sidled into the Campalia's space. He smiled reassuringly at Nilo and politely cleared his throat.

"Um, Comrade Lieutenant? Begging your pardon?"

"What is it, Armas?"

"I couldn't help but overhear. About your papa, ma'am. Er. Comrade Lieutenant."

He approached Costan, eyed him closely, lifted an arm, and pushed it back down when it didn't fall on its own. "Nilo

Costanovich, you were not joking. So." He turned back to Lilya and put on a bright smile. "Where are we going?" He winced inside at his obviously forced nonchalance.

"Don't concern yourself, Armas," Lilya countered distractedly as she continued to flip pages. "We aren't going anywhere."

"We need to get to Jedric Orianos," Nilo interjected. "But we don't have a plane."

Lilya fixed her brother with a stare that was as cold as a Siberian Christmas. Attended by a witches' coven.

"Oh. Well, we . . ." Armas swallowed and pushed on before he could think about what he was saying. "We could take the *Forerunner*, Comrade Lieutenant. If you needed."

"See, Lilya? Even Armas agrees!"

"Armas!" Lilya's tone was scandalized. "Are you suggesting we defy protocol? *You,* of all people, *Comrade Engineer?*"

Armas' thoughts skittered through the animal parts of his brain, trying to decide if it was to be fight, or flight, but in the cramped deer-trail of that part of his psyche he found a Well-Dressed Man watching him.

"Well, no, Comrade Lieutenant. Not in so many words."

"In *what* words, then?"

"We can call it 'approach practice'. Just . . . on a zeppelin."

"A *foreign* zeppelin." She turned to face him fully. "Who's going to get arrested when it goes wrong?"

"Not to worry!" It was beyond too late to stop now. "I will file for an extended navigation exercise."

"All the way to the *Spirit Walker*?"

"It will be even farther if we wait a few more days until we get back to Moscow. We can always say something malfunctioned. The plane is brand new, after all."

He smoothed down bubbled paint on the left cowling.

"There's still a few bugs to work out."

Lilya appeared completely flummoxed. "I do not believe this. From you."

Armas wasn't sure *he* did, either. "Yes, ma'am. But . . . it's your papa."

"I had no idea you were so sentimental." She jabbed a stiff finger at him. "You keep out of it. You're not helping." She turned back to Nilo. "We are *not* taking the plane."

"But we'd just be going up to an airship, asking some questions . . ."

Lilya snatched up her flight bag from the floor and began emptying it onto the workbench.

"Lilya, please!" Nilo begged. "We need to see Jedric—"

"*Nyet!*" She dumped out the rest of her bag and stopped, leaning over the bench with her head bowed.

Armas caught Nilo's eye and offered an encouraging smile.

Nilo took a breath. "Lilya, there's something else . . . . There was a man at the hospital watching Papa."

Lilya exhaled loudly. "What makes you think he was watching him?"

"Expensive suit, acted puffed up. He was loitering around the ward, and then he was on the street outside when I left."

"Family member."

"He left in a black sedan."

"Hospital director."

"With another man dressed exactly the same."

She said nothing, but her shoulders visibly tightened.

Armas couldn't stand the tension. "Don't agents come in threes? One to write notes—"

"Armas . . ." Lilya warned.

"One to read them—"

"*Armas . . .*"

"—and one to watch the two intellectuals . . ." His voice trailed off uncertainly.

"Nilo. Did you speak to him? What did he do? Get annoyed? Tell you to run along?"

"No. He just . . . smiled."

Lilya shoved the bag away and rubbed her forehead tiredly. "Secret Police. Outstanding. My own *father*." She looked at Costan, still standing where he had been left. "Well, this changes things."

Nilo's voice was small, as if he were ashamed of his victory. "They're going to ask questions . . . we're going to need answers. Before then."

Lilya growled, grabbed her bag and began repacking it. "Armas!"

"Comrade Lieutenant!"

"Expedite the repairs. Get the ship pre-flighted."

Nilo sagged with relief. "Thank you, Lilya."

"Nilo." Her voice was again the commanding bark of an officer in charge. "You realize what can happen? If they do not believe our landing there was accidental? You do know?"

"Yes." His answer was subdued, but his eyes had a resolute gleam in them. "But we must help Papa."

"Then get your things. Be back here in an hour."

VII

THE WELL-DRESSED MAN leaned against the fender of the sedan and watched Lilya's car, driven by the boy with the old man inside, drive away.

His companion stood by the sedan's driver's door and watched as well, then turned to his superior. "Sir?" There was a hesitant apprehension in his voice. "You know that engineer is the Commissar General's brother-in-law."

"Of course I do." There were no misgivings in the voice of the Well-Dressed Man. "But once the Conductor is mine the Commissar General will be begging to thank me." He reached through the open window in the rear door, grabbed a small package off the seat, and handed it to the other agent.

"Wait until the Commissar General's brother-in-law is busy filing the flight plan. And don't be seen."

The agent nodded, took the bundle, and slinked off toward the hangar.

Nilo set a well-worn suitcase on the ground and regarded his new ride, parked outside on the tarmac, gleaming in the sun.

The *Forerunner* looked different out here, at once smaller by comparison to the endless sky above, and at the same time larger than life as the import of what he was about to do started sinking in. The Apostolov technicians were conspicuously absent. Lilya sat in the forward cockpit, going through checklists and making a point of ignoring Nilo, so he took the chance to examine the craft more closely. His attention was drawn to the nacelle on the wing. He stepped closer . . .

Armas appeared over his shoulder. "Careful, Nilo. That's top secret."

Nilo nodded and stepped back, taking in a more general view. "No propeller. So this is the nuclear engine. How does it work?" He eyeballed the scorch marks streaked down the length of the housing. "It does work, yes?"

Armas sniffed as if he had been personally insulted. "Of course it does."

Nilo shook his head. "I can't believe they put them in an airplane. You'd think they'd use it to . . . I don't know, power a city or something."

Armas looked chagrined. "Larger units have been unstable."

"I don't recall hearing about—"

"You won't." Armas pushed his glasses up his nose and gave Nilo a leave-it-alone look. "Like I said . . . *'Top Secret'.*"

Nilo could just about hear the capitalization in Armas' voice. And with that, the import of what he was about to do weighed Nilo's gut a little more heavily. "So," he continued, with forced indifference, "where do we sit in this thing?"

Armas climbed up a ladder to a small hatch between the two cockpits and swung it open to reveal a deep, cramped space. "I installed seats in the mail hold."

"Oh . . . so we're steerage?"

"I'm very sorry, Nilo," Lilya finally spoke up from the front cockpit. "but there's nowhere else to put you. The *Forerunner* is built for high-speed mail runs, not holiday joyrides." There was all the sweetness in her voice of a double-shot of espresso. She snapped closed the storage drawer of her clipboard and stowed it in a side pocket on the cockpit wall. "Armas, get the gun."

Armas nodded, slid down the ladder, and opened a crate that Nilo had not previously noticed sitting on the ground next to the plane. He pulled out a hefty-looking piece of hardware and a belt of ammunition and started back up the ladder.

"Hey," Nilo started. "That's a ShKAS—you're not expecting *that* kind of trouble, are you?"

"Live each day as if it's your last," Armas grunted from where he was lifting the gun onto its pintle. "One day you'll be right!"

"Why wouldn't we be expecting trouble?" Lilya challenged as she climbed down to inspect the wings. "The *Spirit Walker* has been over the Inar Gulf for the last week."

"Isn't that a hot area?" Nilo suddenly felt the doubt tapeworm itself a little further into his gut. "Why would Jedric even be there? And why would people go to meet him there?"

Armas locked the gun in place and fed in the ammo belt. "The rich and powerful don't concern themselves with fluff like an imminent war."

"Disputed airspace does tend to keep authority at arms' length," Lilya agreed. "But nevertheless, as far as us going in there, the *Forerunner* is an advanced design."

"No one else has anything like her," Armas said as he slid back down the ladder. He paused on the ground to stroke the metal fuselage lovingly. "No one. Not even the Fritzes."

Lilya rolled her eyes at his display. "Someone with more daring than scruples might want to get hold of her. Inar, for example—"

"Yes, yes, yes!" Nilo fussed. "The Inar secession is all over the news. Troops massing at the border and all."

"By the time we get there that border could very well be in flames."

Armas eyed Nilo with concern. "Brother, you don't look well."

Lilya stopped in the middle of checking the ailerons. "Second thoughts, Nilo?"

Nilo shook himself. He needed to know. "No. None whatever. All aboard." He stepped back to the car and guided Costan across the tarmac, and with some difficulty and help from Armas, up the ladder and into the jury-rigged seat.

He stowed his bag under his own seat and settled in, and Armas shut the hatch over him and scrambled into the aft cockpit.

Lilya finished her circuit around the plane, climbed up to the pilot's seat, and strapped in. She took a last look around to satisfy herself that no one else was around.

"*Clear!*" she called loudly, and Armas ignited the starboard engine.

It growled for a moment, then settled into a low thrum as the revs spooled up. He fired up the portside unit and the *Forerunner* began throbbing with raw power.

Lilya set her goggles over her face, slid the canopy closed, and keyed her intercom. "*Everyone set?*"

Armas checked his gauges. "Coolant, shielding, and output are all go, Comrade Lieutenant."

"Baggage is checked!" Nilo chimed in.

He could hear Lilya sigh over the intercom. "*Nilo,*" she began, but the hard edge had gone out of her voice. "*I know you're expecting answers. Do not be disappointed if there are none. We see what we can and get home again, right?"*

"Right, Lilya." He swallowed the fear down. "But let's hope."

"We are taking our lives into our own hands. I will leave hope to you."

She advanced the throttles and the plane rolled down the taxiway.

Just inside the airfield's perimeter fence, the Well-Dressed Man watched the *Forerunner* depart.

Down the line of hangars, his counterpart appeared from between two buildings and gave a thumbs-up before heading for the sedan parked nearby.

The Well-Dressed Man nodded an acknowledgment, but turned and jogged in the opposite direction to where spinning props could be seen waiting.

VIII

THE SKY was heavy with leaden clouds over the bleak shore of the Inar Gulf. The low ceiling threatened rain and difficult flying, and Lilya kept a close eye on it as she cruised the *Forerunner* sedately along the coast. She was using the strand as a handrail of sorts to navigate to the checkpoint at the Farlind Bluffs from where she would, with any luck, somehow contrive permission to strike out over the water in search of the *Spirit Walker*.

Just above the gravelly beachhead, a rough country road paralleled the bank. At the moment the normally desolate track was crowded with vehicles from cargo trucks to farmer's carts, whose occupants looked up mournfully as the *Forerunner* cruised by. Their own progress forward was stalled—on their landward side battalions of soldiers readying for the call to march into Inar were hard at work converting an empty meadow into an impromptu airfield and staging area, and had set the checkpoint across the route to prevent access—or escape.

Lilya circled the *Forerunner* overhead and took her place in the queue of transports and recon planes in the landing pattern. When her turn came to alight she set deftly down and taxied to a distant, empty corner of the field, far away from overly-inquisitive official eyes.

The engines wound down in a vaporous whine as the *Forerunner*'s front and rear canopies slid open. Lilya climbed down and started shrugging out of her flight suit as Armas paused to watch faint whisps of steam from the left cowling.

"That was a solid extended run, Comrade Lieutenant," he beamed as he joined her on the ground. "Even if it was only at fifty-six percent power." He popped a maintenance cover and removed the boarding ladder.

Lilya settled her service cap on her head. "Did you finally replace that converter with those tractor parts?"

Armas stopped, eyes wide, and broke into a proud smile. "Comrade Lieutenant! You very nearly made a joke!" He looked wistfully at the engines. "But I've never seen full power. I wonder what it's like?"

Lilya donned her flight jacket and looked across the field to the sprawling command tent in the distance under a large red flag snapping in the wind.

"Stay here with them, Armas."

"But—Comrade Lieutenant! *I* always file the flight plans," the engineer protested. "Won't you filing it make the brass curious? It's . . . unusual," he finished lamely, lacking a better word.

"Yes, it will. And you're right, it *is* unusual. But this is practically a war zone." She eyed the milling civilians outside the hastily-erected perimeter fence. "Everything about this is unusual. We'll have some latitude, but it will take rank to take advantage of it."

Armas still looked doubtful. "They say there's nothing so dangerous as a junior officer with a plan . . . . You be careful, Comrade Lieutenant."

Lilya jabbed a knife-hand gesture toward the mail bay. "You just make sure those two don't get into any trouble."

Lilya marched smartly past army officers exchanging forms, signatures, and salutes as they prepared to advance their respective units through the checkpoint to forward areas. From the gate to the command tent a line of desperately tired civilians shifted from one foot to another, each man, woman, and child of them apprehensively waiting their turn to explain why they were non-combatants who needed to be long gone from the area on the eve of war.

Everywhere along the path, piles of cast-off personal things too burdensome to carry further stood in forlorn contrast to the neatly ordered crates of supplies and stacks of rifles and rucksacks.

At the command tent's entrance Lilya joined a shorter line of army personnel. Though there were fewer people in front of her, shadows still seemed to lengthen steadily as she crept forward.

At last, she found herself at a camp desk manned by a tired corporal. He looked up but there was little interest in his eyes as he asked, "Purpose for entering Inar, Comrade Lieutenant?"

She brandished Armas' flight plan. "Extended navigation exercise."

He took the paper and examined it briefly. His expression didn't even change. "I'll have to clear this with the Captain. One moment, ma'am." He waved to a gruff-looking older officer grumbling sourly over the shoulder of a private into a radio mouthpiece. The officer scowled and handed the mike back to the radio operator, then strode over impatiently.

"What?"

The corporal handed him the flight plan. "Captain Kurtikova, Lieutenant Campalia. She's with the *Forerunner*, sir. On a navigation flight."

Kurtikova looked up from the paper with skepticism in his eye. "Over the Inar Gulf?"

"We are testing our navigation gear, sir. We need to be over open water."

"Anyone riding escort for you in case you get lost?"

"No, sir. We had none to spare." She nodded to the build-up behind her. "That's why we came here, in fact. No escort to just head out over the Arctic."

Kurtikova shook his head. "You do realize this entire region is about to become a battleground?" He waved to the soldiers drilling in the open field. "I'm pretty sure they do." He waved next to the worried civilians. "And I know for a fact they do."

"With all due respect, Comrade Captain, all the more reason to complete our testing now."

Kurtikova frowned and handed the flight plan back. "I'm sorry, Lieutenant, but no. The Inar have obtained anti-aircraft capable submarines and they have already been spotted operating in the vicinity."

"But sir! This is all that's left of our testing program!"

"I said *Nyet,* Comrade Lieutenant."

Kurtikova turned to leave. Lilya hesitated, not sure what to do next. Curse Nilo for dragging her into this, and curse her father for getting himself into whatever this really was! Now she was committed, with a very expensive and high-profile piece of gear on an unscheduled flight in a restricted area with a lame excuse for even being here. Never mind what Armas claimed. Sure, he had leeway with the testing schedule, but did he have *that* much slack to justify something like this? Now what? Just take off over the gulf? She had walked past an entire squadron of fighters parked on the flightline on her way to this desk and even though she could outrun them, where would she go if she did? She wouldn't be able to stop at the *Spirit Walker*. Inar? Sweden? Great Britain? And with the Secret Police involved, would anywhere be safe?

All these thoughts raced through her head in an instant and were brought up short when the desk phone rang.

The corporal picked it up. "Yes?"

Suddenly he sat bolt upright. "Oh! Certainly, sir!" He reached back for Kurtikova's elbow who, in the half-heartbeat that had passed since his refusal, had only managed to get a single step away. "Sir?"

The captain turned as if to rebuke the man but stopped when he saw the nervous look on his face. He took the phone receiver and put it to his ear. "What? I'm busy." He glared at Lilya as he listened, then rolled his eyes and handed the phone back to the corporal. When he spoke, it was as if someone was dragging him around by his close-cropped hair. "Wait here, Lieutenant."

He strutted to a desk far to the rear of the tent where an athletic man in a tailored suit and fedora waited. They conversed, and judging by the captain's stance, it was not a pleasant exchange.

Lilya watched them with a keen interest. She caught the eye of the corporal. "Who's that man? The well-dressed one in civilian clothes?"

The corporal was trying to look as if he had nothing to do with anything, but the sudden scowl on his face, like he had eaten something foul, gave him away. "Secret Police," he spat in a low voice. "Just walked in a bit ago, like he owned the place."

"Some would say they do," Lilya observed dryly, and was rewarded with a helpless frown from the corporal.

In the back of the tent, the Well-Dressed Man tipped his hat. It was a congenial enough gesture though the shadows hid his face, and Lilya was willing to wager his expression was more predatory than philanthropic. He exited the tent and Kurtikova marched back to where Lilya was waiting, scowling even harder than before.

"Give me that flight plan."

She handed it back, he stamped it, signed it, and thrust it back to her. "You have six hours. That's all. I can't guarantee your safety beyond that. Not that I can now, but—"

Lilya plucked the flight plan out of his hand and offered a hasty salute. "More than enough, sir, thank you." She turned and jogged out of the tent before he could change his mind.

Lilya stuffed the flight plan into a pocket of her coverall. She wasn't sure what she felt about it all. Breaking protocol was one thing, operating completely without orders was something else, and deceiving a superior officer was . . .

Well, she didn't want to think about where *that* could lead. It was frigid, lonely, and hungry.

But on the other hand, if what Nilo said was true and the Secret Police actually were involved, this whole situation would probably end up there anyway. Even if she did nothing she very well could end up in a very cold shed in a very distant place. So may as well do something . . .

Secret Police . . . a Well-Dressed Man that had been loitering around the hospital ward . . .

She didn't recall seeing anyone like that herself when she had been there, but then she had only been on the floor for a short while and hadn't been looking. But her mysterious benefactor matched, at least in a basic sense, her brother's description of Costan's shadow. Though why he would have intervened *on* her behalf she couldn't fathom. That made her uncomfortable. She didn't like unknown variables. As a pilot one didn't fly if too many things were out of sorts, and her alarm bells were starting to go off in spades. She needed to find out more.

By the time she stepped out into the indifferent sunlight, she had made up her mind. In for a penny, in for a pound, she had heard once on a childhood tour in Piccadilly Circus. She took an immediate left and circled around to see if she could find this curious player, and maybe by watching him gain some insight into his motives.

On her way past a pile of discarded goods she snatched up an overlarge topcoat and a floppy workman's hat. Best to be inconspicuous, she reasoned, and threw them on over her uniform.

On the far side of the tent, she caught sight of him heading down the line of supply crates toward the airfield. He was scanning around, obviously on the lookout for pursuit. Just like an agent, Lilya thought. Doing it out of habit. When he turned her way she stopped and became suddenly very interested in an empty trunk.

He changed course then and headed for the checkpoint gate. Lilya slipped behind a tractor, shucked the cap, put on her sunglasses, and let down her hair.

When she stepped out again a group of dispirited teens in dark brown uniform dresses were passing by, following in line behind a school matron waving a flag. She fell in behind them and monitored her quarry as he doubled back.

When the schoolgirls headed off in another direction Lilya ducked again between two supply tents, snatched up a shawl, and dropped her glasses to her nose. By now the Well-Dressed Man was heading back toward the command tent again. At the entrance he stopped and waited calmly. She adopted a frustrated frown and limped away.

Her frown was not entirely feigned.

A short while later Lilya was back in uniform and striding across the airfield to the *Forerunner*. Following the

Well-Dressed Man had accomplished little aside from confirming he was, in fact, an agent of the Secret Police. But what was really going on, and most especially why did he appear to help her, was still a very big unknown.

She marched along, arms folded, watching the ground and trying to puzzle out what it all meant, when she accidentally came up behind two low-ranking soldiers. They were grumbling as they dawdled to avoid getting back to their duties.

"I'm telling you, Yaromir, it's about time we got some action. I'm tired of drilling all the time and not doing anything."

"I don't know, brother," the one called Yaromir answered uncertainly. "I don't much like the idea of shooting our own."

Lilya took a quick look around and stepped up close behind Yaromir. "You need to be more careful in front of the commissars, Private," she offered helpfully.

The young man's head snapped around at her voice, then followed her nod toward an aloof middle-aged woman with the black-piped rank badges of a senior *politruk* overseeing the sorting of supplies not far away.

"Oh, yes, Comrade Lieutenant . . ." the youth stammered. "I only meant to say that—"

"She won't care what you *meant* to say, Private. Not by half."

The other soldier stopped short. "Hey!" He pointed out over the water on the far side of the perimeter fence and its clustered civilians. "What's that?"

Lilya turned and her heart sank, to be quickly replaced by an adrenaline rush as her fighting instincts flared.

The water bubbled as if it were boiling, and an instant later a dull gray ship emblazoned with the blue-cross-on-a-white-field of the presumptive Inar state surged up out of the waves.

It was built vaguely along the lines of the Kaiser's submersible boats of the Great War, but was larger, with a bulky, canister-shaped superstructure ahead of the main sail. As the sub settled into a level attitude clamshell doors opened in the ship's container and two small craft sprung out on rails. Folded wings dropped and charges fired, catapulting the two diminutive planes into the air over the dumbfounded civilians.

A second later sirens blared overhead, and across the airfield Soviet pilots scrambled to their own fighters. Engines coughed, spit oily smoke, and roared into the air to engage the newcomers.

Lilya and the two privates ducked close to the ground and ran for the cover of the supply caches.

"What is a sub doing here?" Yaromir asked Lilya.

As if she knew, she thought. "It can't be just scouting the border. Not alone like this—"

One Inar plane dived low to the ground and buzzed the command tent belching scores of leaflets that fell over the civilians like so many moths. Some people ran for cover but a few reached for the elusive strips of paper.

Kurtikova charged out of the tent, face livid. "Drop those papers! That's Inar propaganda!"

Overhead tracers streaked as the Red fighters engaged the Inar craft. Some of the civilians cried in terror, some cheered at the sight, but they all dived for cover when stray rounds peppered the ground.

A fuel truck exploded and everyone scattered.

Lilya clapped the two privates on their shoulders. "Good luck!" she yelled and bolted for the *Forerunner*. She waved her arms as she ran until she got Armas' attention from where he was watching the skies fearfully. "Fire it up, Armas! Get the engines going!"

Flak rounds burst in the air as the sub's deck guns opened up on the harassing Red aircraft. The Inar plane that dropped the leaflets struck out over the gulf, using the antiaircraft fire for cover now that its mission was complete.

The second Inar craft dodged and maneuvered to escape from his pursuers, but it was no use. Tracers marked a deadly trail from one of the Red plane's guns and the Inar ship began trailing smoke. It descended, barely under control, and as it flared for a forced landing a final burst from the Soviet hunter threw it into the ground in a smoking, twisted pile.

Lilya's pace slackened as she watched a stumbling figure swathed in flames emerge from the wreckage, collapse to the ground, and lay still.

In the distance the loitering Inar sub turned for open water, closing its compartment doors and slipping under the waves to the sound of a blaring klaxon horn.

Lilya reached the *Forerunner* and climbed into the cockpit. Armas was frozen in the act of securing the mail hold hatch over Nilo and Costan, watching aghast as the Inar plane burned.

He shook himself and looked up at Lilya. "You look like you just saw a ghost."

She ignored him and snapped her seat belts closed as she looked over her instrument panel to the fallen Inar craft, and the small, huddled, still form alongside.

All around them leaflets continued to fall like hundreds of lily petals.

IX

THE LAST RAYS of the sun danced over the *Forerunner*'s flanks as it cruised high over the gulf. In the far distance, several thousand feet lower and already in the shadow of the earth's horizon, the *Spirit Walker* began to light up with powerful floodlamps on its upper deck, floating among the clouds like an electric vision of some Nordic god.

Within the plane, everyone was silent as Lilya closed on the giant airship. She set the airship's frequency on the radio and keyed the mike.

"*Spirit Walker*, this is Apostolov Delta One Three Zero. We are ten kilometers east, inbound with engine trouble, requesting permission to come aboard, over."

"*One Three Zero, this is* Spirit Walker," a reassuring female voice crackled over her headphones. "*Permission granted. Stand by for our windward turn.*"

Nilo looked out the small window in the mail hold hatch as the *Forerunner* banked to line up with the airship. On the water far below, he could just make out the luminescent wakes of corvettes out of Morograd searching for the Inar submarine.

Within a matter of minutes Lilya had set them down on the *Spirit Walker*'s flight deck. A ground crewman directed her to cut the engines and a tractor scooted up, latched onto the nosewheel, and towed them to an elevator that brought them down a level to the expansive hangar deck.

The four occupants exited the plane by their various routines as loudspeakers echoed overhead. Miles of glass panes lined the walls, admitting shafts of sunlight reflecting off high clouds into the echoing aluminum cavern. Bustling activity was everywhere as maintenance crews swarmed back and forth servicing a varied flock of civilian aircraft ranging from ancient stick-and-wire jobs to the latest stressed-skin aluminum frames.

As Armas fussed over his post-shutdown checklist and Nilo guided Costan clear of the hot engines, Lilya took in the aeronautical commotion with professional interest.

Her eyes alighted on a youngish, elegantly-dressed gentleman approaching shadowed by an older uniformed man with a bland expression on a mousy face. The pair stopped before her and the younger man thrust out a hand.

"Welcome!" he enthused. "I am Jedric Orianos, master of the *Spirit Walker*!"

Lilya shook his hand in a businesslike manner. "Lieutenant Lilya Campalia, Soviet Military Air Forces Special Unit."

Jedric looked past her at the *Forerunner*, admiring the sleek crimson metalwork. "And what have we here? Fascinating craft!" He was bubbling incredulity. "This couldn't possibly be the new—"

"I'm afraid I cannot say," Lilya cut him off, brow arched significantly.

Jedric paused, then broke into a ready but knowing smile. "Of course, of course! But certainly, you would introduce me to your companions?"

"Of course." She half-turned to Armas, who had finished securing the plane and was stepping up to his customary place on her left hand. "This is my Chief Engineer Losily Armas. And this is my brother Nilo . . . and my father, Costan Campalia, the eminent escape artist."

"You know him already—" Nilo challenged.

"Nilo!" Lilya snapped.

Jedric shook hands with Armas and Nilo, but seemed put off by Costan's blank expression. "Charmed, very charmed," he offered, recovering quickly. "But no, Lieutenant, think nothing of it. Of course, I've heard of your father. We've even played at the same venues from time to time, over the years."

Nilo shot his sister a smug look behind Jedric's back as the performer turned his attention back to the *Forerunner*.

"Naturally our maintenance facilities will be at your complete disposal. We will be happy to assist—"

"Thank you, sir, but no." Lilya's voice was as calm and unmoved as the tundra. "Armas will stay here and handle all our repairs." She scanned the activity around them, eager to change the subject. "Besides, it looks like you have your hands full already. Quite a gathering you have here tonight."

"Yes, we've a séance this evening." At least Jedric appeared just as willing as Lilya to get off the topic of the *Forerunner*.

"Even with the Inar situation?"

"It *has* been months in the planning," the medium explained.

Now it was Armas' turn to give Nilo a smug look behind Jedric's back.

If Jedric was aware of the goings-on, he gave no sign. "In any case, in light of your circumstances, I suspect you will be requiring a more private setting for your craft?"

"That is essential," Lilya replied.

"Of course, Lieutenant. I will have your ship moved to the aft deck and curtained off. In the meantime, shall we?" He indicated a bank of elevators some distance away and began walking toward them.

Lilya nodded to Armas, who hung back as Nilo took Costan by the elbow and fell into line behind Lilya, Jedric, and his mouse-faced companion.

As they reached the elevator doors the deck lurched noticeably. Lilya shot a look back at the *Forerunner*, still sitting unmoved where she had left it, and then to Jedric, who looked slightly chagrined.

"With how the weather is turning our little ritual tonight will be . . . interesting, to say the least."

The doors opened, the officer and the Campalias entered, but Jedric hung back. "Master Perun will accompany you to take care of your accommodations while your man repairs your ship," he explained.

Nilo looked puzzled. "You're coming with us, aren't you?"

"I fear my presence will be required in the sessorium shortly. But please, enjoy your stay. I hope to see you again before you leave."

Perun threw the handle to close the doors. "You can count on it!" Nilo called as Jedric disappeared from their view.

"Nilo!" Lilya's irritation was clearly evident.

"What?"

"Remember we were not invited here." She folded her arms, for all the world looking like a mother ashamed of an errant toddler.

Nilo sulked and turned away, taking an interest in the woven wall of the elevator and the passing shadows showing through.

He looked closer and reached out to touch it. "Hey—is this fabric?"

Perun's voice was the patient and even tone of a trained hospitality professional. "All the bulkheads are fabric, young sir, for lightness."

After a few more rather long, awkward, and silent moments, the elevator stopped and the doors opened on an elegantly-appointed passageway that looked more like an art deco hotel than a ship's corridor. At random intervals down its length soigné guests were leaning over door locks, letting themselves into their staterooms, and gasping at the sight as their portals opened.

Perun led them a hundred feet down the hall, stopped before a door, unlocked it, and handed them a key. "This will be your stateroom, complements of Mr. Orianos. We are one deck above the dining salon, which can be reached by the stairwell just there," he nodded to a brass-chased door a little further down the hall.

Lilya stepped over the threshold and instantly saw why the other patrons had been amazed. Like the hangar deck above, large windows angled outward and downward filled the far wall of the compartment and offered a stunning view of the moon rising over the gulf. Here, though, the windows weren't five meters in the air, they were at waist level. She reached out, turned the latch on one pane, and opened it. Cool air breezed in with the scent of fresh water and distant rain. The effect was rather dizzying and she shut the window quickly. As her eyes swept the rest of the chamber she noted sleek overstuffed couches of modern design, and—

"Scented candles?" she remarked, taken aback. "There are no flame restrictions?" Like everyone she was mindful of the tragedy that had befallen the *Hindenburg*. The fact that it had happened in the United States had been no hindrance to making the official news channels coming out of Moscow; in fact, the Kremlin had seemed eager to point out how neither Roosevelt's capitalist industrialist cronies nor the national socialist zealots of Hitler's Germany had been able to prevent the disaster.

"We use helium for lift, Lieutenant," Perun explained patiently. "There is no fire hazard here."

"Impressive," Lilya admitted, "and expensive."

"Only the best for our guests, ma'am. Will there be anything else?"

"Thank you, no."

"Very good, then, ma'am." Perun offered a half bow and departed.

Nilo waited until he was well gone down the passageway before muttering, "What, no warning to stay in our rooms and ignore any odd sounds we hear tonight?"

"Nilo!" Lilya said again, but this time her voice was only weary.

"What? I'm just saying . . ." He shook his head and led Costan into the stateroom and set him down on one of the couches. He, though, paced restlessly. "So how are we going to find anything out? This thing is huge."

Lilya opened the refrigerator and withdrew two bottles of spring water. She opened one for herself and handed the other to Nilo with a nod to try to give it to Costan. "Do you still have Father's tools?"

Nilo dutifully withdrew the wallet from his jacket pocket.

"This ship is mostly empty space," she continued. "We dropped at least fifty meters from the hangar deck. There has to be a way to access it."

"What are we going to find there?"

"A way to move around where no one will see. Did you bring anything black in that suitcase of yours?"

X

LILYA AND NILO scrambled along narrow catwalks in the dimly-lit vastness of the interior of the airship. Just overhead loomed expansive gasbags defined by guy wires and supported by fretted girders that, despite their obvious strength, seemed delicate enough that gripping one too tightly would be enough to crumple it.

Below them a perforated screen allowed a view into a large well-appointed cabaret that spanned the entire salon deck. A single waitress was busily setting tables, humming a cheery tune to herself as she worked.

"Wow," Nilo quipped, unable to help himself. "That's the dining room?" He'd seen some posh digs in his travels with his Papa, but what he saw below him was in a class by itself.

"Shh!" Lilya hissed. "No unnecessary talking!"

As if to prove her point, the waitress looked up, brow creased in puzzlement.

Nilo slipped back a step though he knew the girl most likely couldn't see anything in the dark recesses of the ship above the well-lit salon. Still, there had been something about her, something unnerving and familiar that tickled the back of his brain for an instant. But then it was gone. He shook himself and slinked back to Lilya's shoulder. "Okay. So where would this 'sessorium' be?"

"Where a showman would be able to get the most dramatic view. In the nose."

"Right. How do we get up there?"

"Do I look like I have the blueprints?" She was getting testy. "Start looking around. You go that way, I'll go this."

They split up. Nilo didn't like being alone, especially here, and nearly getting caught right at the beginning of their exploration didn't help.

He bit back an indignant retort and struck off forward.

Lilya pushed onward, trying to keep her bearings in the maze of lattice-work braces and struts.

A cold breeze ruffled a stray hair and she followed it. It seemed to be coming from aft, where the passenger accommodations gave way to more service-oriented areas. This wasn't going to lead to some private room where the well-heeled could lose their money to a charlatan, she knew, but she was curious what it *could* be.

After a few more moments' search she found it: a large, framed opening gaping in the airship's underside. Glittering clouds passed below like so many snowdrifts.

She looked up, wondering, and suspecting, what could require such a portal, and she was not disappointed.

A fat little barrel of a plane with a whopping round engine and long protruding guns hung on a sturdy hook, poised nose-down over the gap.

Why did Jedric Orianos need a fighter plane? Granted, he seemed prone to hanging out in sketchy locations, but usually bringing a weapon to a party without knowing how to use it was more dangerous than being unarmed, and Jedric struck her as being a savvy individual, not some posturing rube.

But that would mean . . .

She turned and headed quickly back the way she had come.

"Lilya!" Nilo called from a service door. "There you are!" His voice was heavy with relief. "This way!"

Lilya calmed her own racing pulse and followed Nilo through the door. He led her to a spiral framework stair running from unseen depths below into the darkness above, and pointed up.

As they climbed the sound of the airship's droning engines became gradually less audible, to be replaced in stages by the cold wind rushing over the outer envelope. At last, they reached a level where bracing wires radiated out from central rings in all directions—the longitudinal axis. They took a catwalk forward another hundred yards until they could just make out a sizable tent-like chamber lit from within by faint, shifting glows.

A gust of wind shook the ship's frame and rattled the catwalk. They crouched down, more out of fear of falling than of being seen, and stepped lightly onto the platform surrounding the room.

Nilo stopped short and pointed ahead to where Lilya could see dark-clad figures moving around the sessorium, pulling wires and making suggestive noises.

"I told you this spiritualist business was garbage," she whispered. "Come on." They circled around the other way to an unoccupied side where a slightly brighter light marked a peephole the size of a person's hand.

"Here, Nilo. This must be so the stagehands can follow along." They crowded close and watched.

Inside, the room was draped in dark fabric. Jedric sat at the head of a candlelit table littered with occult paraphernalia, speaking softly in a droning voice that appeared to be answered by the mysterious sounds from outside the walls as objects floated into view to the excited whispers of the patrons. Behind Jedric an immense circular window showed the moonlight, breathtaking through the cloud cover, lending a perfectly unearthly cast to the scene.

Ursula stood watch on the *Spirit Walker*'s bridge. Beneath her feet, the deck pitched in the gathering storm.

The weather officer looked up from his radio table, littered with charts and notes, eyes worried. "Ma'am? The weather's only getting worse."

Ursula's response was even. "Are we clear at higher altitudes?"

"For the time being, ma'am."

"Very well," she sighed, regarding the dramatic moonlight. "Too bad about the séance, but safety first. Helm, take us up to three thousand meters."

Lilya elbowed Nilo in the ribs. "Nilo. Nilo! Wake up!"

"What . . . what?" He shook himself, then clutched the floor as another gust shook the ship and the deck angled noticeably upward.

"You dozed off," Lilya explained. "What's with you?"

"It's his voice . . . it puts you to sleep."

And abruptly things made a little more sense to Lilya. "He must be using some kind of hypnosis to enhance the stage effects." Despite herself she had to admire Orianos' cleverness. She turned back to the peephole again.

Through the window over Jedric's shoulder, the clouds could be seen falling away as the *Spirit Walker* attained smoother air. The moon broke through, clear, silver, and—

Shining directly onto the peephole.

Lilya gasped and ducked, pulling Nilo down as well.

"What?" Nilo asked, again afraid.

"He saw me. We have to go."

They emerged from the bowels of the ship through another small service door in an alcove off the stateroom deck passageway, at the opposite end from the elevators.

Nilo made to step out into the hall but Lilya pulled him back and peeked around the corner.

Jedric was waiting patiently by their stateroom door.

"How did he—" Nilo began, craning around her.

"Who cares?" she snapped under her breath. "Give me the lockpicks."

"What? Why should I?"

"Better for me to be caught with them than you."

"Why?" he demanded as he pulled the wallet from his pocket.

"Because I can lie better. Hand them over."

A moment later they stepped out into the passageway and walked up to Jedric as if nothing were out of the ordinary.

"Hello," he greeted them amiably. "May I see you in your stateroom?"

Lilya adopted a bemused expression. "Is there a problem?"

"Oh, nothing serious. Please, inside." He opened the door for them and ushered them in.

Once they were all in the room, he eased the door closed and locked it, then stepped close to Lilya, took her hand, and squeezed it while he stared intently into her eyes.

"Hello. I am Jedric . . ."

"I know who you—"

"—and you . . . are asleep."

He gently let go of her hand and Lilya remained fixed in position, mouth open and hand extended.

Nilo was at once amazed, afraid, and impressed. "You really *are* a hypnotist! You put her under that fast?" On the downside, he realized at that moment he was completely in the medium's power. *His* ship. *His* crew. And the only person that could get him out of here was rooted in place like a mannequin.

Suddenly coming here seemed like it had been a really bad idea. "Lilya?"

"She will not hear you."

The fear took over now. "What are you doing to her?"

Jedric held up his hands. "Easy, lad. I truthfully mean you no harm. Besides, I can't make her do anything against her will."

"You made those old biddies up there think they were talking to the dead," he countered, reasoning that trying to hide where they had been was now completely useless.

Jedric nodded and touched his finger to the side of his nose. "Which they wanted to believe. Have no fear, I will release her in a moment. But first . . ." He turned to Lilya, folded his arms, and his voice took on a stern tone. "Lieutenant. You will hear me?"

"Yes." Her voice was as distant as her expression.

"Good. Now listen carefully. You *want* to tell me the truth. Your honor depends on it . . . . Why are you here?"

"To find out what happened to our father. Costan."

"Why did you bring the *Forerunner*?"

"Civilian flights were grounded. There was a train . . . . It was the only way to get here."

"I see." Nilo was surprised to see Jedric seemed truly puzzled, and this gave him a glimmer of hope that this might not actually turn out with them being locked up in whatever served as a brig on this overstuffed balloon until they could be handed over to the Secret Police. Or Interpol. Or someone.

He snapped out of his gloomy muse when Jedric leaned in close and asked in a whisper, "Lieutenant, this is important. You *must* be truthful . . ."

"Do you know Ion Boyan?"

XI

IN A REMOTE CORNER of the *Spirit Walker's* hangar deck Armas pushed a tool cart through a large curtain.

A moment later there was a muffled *bang!* from within the enclosure and smoke wisped out from under the draped tarpaulin's hem.

In the stateroom Costan became agitated and began trembling. "*Boyan—Boyan—Boyan—Boyan—*" he mumbled with fearful urgency.

Jedric pointed to the wet bar. "Nilo! The akvavit! Quickly now!"

Nilo leaped for the bottle, not even thinking about what all this meant. He popped the cap and pressed it into Jedric's hands, who then held it to Costan's lips and dribbled the liquor into his mouth until he calmed.

Once again in control, Jedric turned back to Lilya who yet remained fixed in her place by the door.

"Lieutenant. Do you know Deputy Ion Boyan?"

"No."

Jedric rocked back on his heel, mulling her response, then passed his hands over her eyes. "In a moment you will awaken feeling refreshed. Three, two, one . . . awake."

Lilya blinked and shook her head. She swayed slightly and Nilo grabbed her by the arm and led her to a chair.

"What . . . just happened?" she said, reaching a hand to her eyes.

Nilo handed her a drink. She sipped doubtfully.

Jedric opened his mouth to speak but before he could there was an urgent knock at the door. He turned and opened it.

Perun was standing there, his normally bland expression replaced by one filled with exigency.

"Begging your pardon, sir." He looked past Jedric to Lilya. "Lieutenant?"

Lilya turned still-slightly-groggy eyes on Perun. "Y— yes?"

"There's been an accident with your aircraft."

Lilya was instantly alert. "Accident?"

Lilya looked over Armas' shoulder at the forward landing gear bay. Structural braces bore angry char marks and hoses dangled loosely, dripping oil.

"What happened?"

Armas wrung his hands. "I was running checks on the Number One engine, there was a bang behind me . . . and this."

She reached into the mess and felt the burned ends of the hoses, touched the blacked aluminum, and sniffed the residue they left on her fingers. "Nothing could have shorted out?'

Armas' expression was hurt.

Lilya frowned. "Then this was deliberate."

"This is going to get us arrested!" Armas wailed.

Lilya gave him a scathing look, then rolled her eyes. "You think so? What will it take to repair?"

"An hour at most. But we'll need parts. We'll have to call for them."

Lilya nodded resolutely. "I will contact Apostolov, tell them we made an emergency landing after the damage occurred. Can you make it look accidental?"

"Can you see Siberia from the Lubyanka Prison basement?"

"Keep your head on, Armas! And keep your eyes open. Things are not right on this ship."

"*You* think so?"

Lilya stood and stepped over to Jedric, who was leaning through the curtain talking to an unseen crewman. "Mr. Orianos? A word."

Jedric dismissed the crewman and turned to her, eyebrows raised. "How is it?"

"Repairable, but we will be calling the manufacturer for support. Which means I can guarantee the Secret Police will be coming with them. Look, Mr. Orianos. I have some questions and I want some answers." She dropped her voice so only he could hear. "I know you paid the bill for my father to stay at the hospital in Morograd. I also believe you know that *I* know you are not in the slightest what you present yourself to be to your patrons. I know the Secret Police had a deliberate hand in allowing me to even be here with the *Forerunner.*" She crossed her arms and gave him an assertive look. "It's time you told me what's going on."

Jedric studied her for a moment, nodded to himself, and pulled her further out of Armas' hearing. "I think you are right. Let me be honest with you. Your young brother mentioned on your arrival that I knew your father. The truth is, we do know each other."

"So Nilo was right. How well?"

"Only professionally. I was quite surprised when he came to me. I presume he's not what one would call a devotee of spiritualism?"

Lilya stifled a laugh. "Not by half."

"As I supposed. In any event, when I saw him, he was at his wit's end. Um . . ." He paused as if he still had lingering doubts about how to go on, but then seemed to reach a decision. "Are you aware your father works for the government?"

This time Lilya laughed out loud. "My father? He's an escape artist!"

"He is also an agent for the Secret Police."

"He is no such thing!"

"No, my dear, think about it!" He half smiled and leaned in conspiratorially. "A favored guest of the highest circles? Free to travel the world? And he an expert in escaping, and thus getting into, locked spaces?"

Lilya's eyes grew wide as she digested the implications. "And every bureaucrat from here to Berlin anxious to show the famous Sublime Costan around their offices to impress their inferiors . . ."

Jedric nodded as she caught up. "He reported directly to Deputy Ion Boyan, Head of the Secret Police in Moroskaya."

"Tell me what you know. All of it."

"As I understand it, three days ago Boyan proposed Costan use you—*you*, Lieutenant, for a mission."

"Me? What sort of mission?"

"To help flush out a smuggler of expatriates. A mysterious figure known only as 'The Conductor', supposedly hiding aboard my ship."

"Human trafficking?" Lilya looked around the shrouded space, empty save for Armas diligently at work removing broken parts from the *Forerunner*. "This is where Armas would crack a joke about making a Russian duet by sending abroad a Russian quartet."

Her sudden levity made Jedric do a double-take.

"What did Father tell him?" she went on.

"He wouldn't allow it, of course. He was trying to protect you."

"I doubt he cared that much."

"I would hazard to disagree. I—forgive me, but—I understand your mother passed away a few years ago?"

Lilya looked askance at Jedric at the sudden change of tack. "There was . . . an accident. We never heard all the details."

"And Costan was not a spiritualist. Yet he came to me to ask me to contact the spirit of your mother Ilse to guide him, to tell him what he should do."

Lilya breathed deep, trying to put it all together. "But how did he come to be in the state he's in?"

Jedric's expression became suddenly apologetic. "Some of this I have only just pieced together since. At the time I hypnotized him, I thought to just say something bland to put his mind at ease. But I didn't know enough . . ."

Lilya bristled at his hesitation. "What exactly did you do, Mr. Orianos?"

"I could only suggest that he see to his duty and protect his family. When I pulled him out . . ."

"We had this." There was a moment of awkward silence. Lilya closed her eyes and took another deep breath. When she looked at Jedric again, she was once more the Officer In Charge. "Then this is your doing, Jedric. What do you think happened?"

"Well, Lieutenant, if I had to speculate . . . would you consider your father a patriot?"

"He loved Moroskaya, as far as I could tell. Though he *was* originally from Inar Province."

Jedric's eyebrows rose.

"Not everyone in Inar is a fan of the secession," Lilya explained. She thought back to the throngs of anxious civilians at the checkpoint. "What are you getting at?"

"When he worked alone, protecting his country protected you as well. On the other hand, Boyan's mission would have risked you, for the sake of the country."

"And you told him to do his duty *and* protect his family."

"I forced an impossible choice. The only way he could cope with the conflict was to mentally step out of it."

"And thus, we have him as he is now. What next?"

"We must resolve the conflict. But I do not yet know how to do that, short of getting Boyan to revoke his assignment."

Lilya considered this and frowned. "So we are at a dead end, and you have nothing else to offer. At least . . . not at the moment." She moved to the curtain and held it open. "Well, Mr. Orianos, the hour is late and I have much to think about. Good night."

Jedric followed and stopped at the flap. He made to shake her hand, but when she took his, he lifted it up and regarded the silver ring on her finger. "Your mother's death cost you an adoring father. Please do not allow anger at losing what he once was consume you."

"I beg your pardon?" She snatched her hand away. "Perhaps I only mourn the apology I will now never hear from him. You are taking liberties, sir."

Jedric hesitated for only a moment. "Of course. I was inexcusably callous." He offered her a half bow. "I beg your forgiveness. Good night."

Early the next morning Nilo followed Lilya and Armas off the elevator onto the wind-blown flight deck to meet a large transport parked just off the main aircraft lift. The recent arrival was marked with the Apostolov Design Bureau logo, and as the three approached similarly-garbed technicians emerged from a large door in the rear of the plane carrying toolboxes and parts containers.

Nilo was still trying to make sense of what Lilya had said the night before. Their father a spy? The idea may have some logical merit, if Jedric could be believed, but really? A *spy?*

He had been trying to get his head around it ever since and hadn't made any progress, and even now was still lost in his bewildered introspections when a raging drone broke overhead. He looked up, startled, to see more than a dozen buzzing rotorcraft emblazoned with the hammer-sickle-and-sword of the Secret Police rising from beneath the *Spirit*

Walker. Several landed and disgorged squads of officers that spread out, securing the deck, more poured belowdecks at a run.

Several officers surrounded Lilya and her companions, who were frozen in confusion at the sudden turn. At a bellowed command from a man with the red epaulets of a sergeant major the ranks snapped to attention and turned to face a small twin-engined craft that had just alighted on the deck and was taxiing to a halt before them.

The craft's engines slowed to an idle and stopped. After a moment a hatch at the rear fuselage opened and a figure stepped out of the shadowy interior into the sunlight.

It was the Well-Dressed Man.

XII

JEDRIC LEANED over the intercom on the *Spirit Walker's* bridge. His brows were knitted together. "Say again, Ursula?"

"*It's the Secret Police, sir,*" came the first officer's tinny voice. "*They're all over us. The passengers are frightened.*"

Ursula stood close by his elbow. "This doesn't sound good, sir."

Jedric's response was characteristically firm. "Send emergency signal three-one-one before they shut down the radios. And make our heading one-five-zero," he said as he grabbed his jacket on his way to the hatchway, "but do it *gently.*"

"You know they'll shut down our engines, too, sir."

"I know." Jedric winked at her. "But you can still sail the wind, can't you?"

On the hangar deck Jedric exited the elevator and stepped smartly up to the Well-Dressed Man, who was holding his hat against the stiff breeze.

"Deputy Boyan, I presume?"

"You must truly be psychic, Mr. Orianos." Boyan said with only a hint of sarcasm. "Thank you for receiving us."

To the side, guarded by the line of officers, Armas caught Lilya's eye. "So much for staying ahead of the authorities," he muttered. "We're done for."

Jedric's smile never left his face. "I must admit I am at a loss why an officer of such rank would take it upon himself to visit me personally."

"Easily enough explained, Mr. Orianos." Boyan oozed. "You have aboard your ship a particular craft we have had in development for some time."

"You mean of course the *Forerunner.*"

"The very same. Walk with me, please." Boyan set a long-legged pace toward the elevators and waved for the officers standing by Lilya, Nilo, and Armas to bring the trio along. "The craft is quite precious to us."

"Harnesses the power of the atom, as they say. Whatever that means."

Boyan seemed perturbed at Jedric's acumen. "Yes, quite. As it was disabled over disputed waters, I thought it prudent to dispatch a complete security team."

"I hardly would have thought it necessary."

Lilya regarded Boyan closely. "Are we under arrest, Comrade Deputy?"

Boyan regarded her with suspicion. "Let us just say it would not be wise to do anything aside from staying with your craft and seeing to its repair, Lieutenant."

Lilya fell back half a step and Armas nudged her elbow. "I hear the hardest ten years in the gulag are the first five," he said weakly. "Then it just gets longer."

"Stay calm," Lilya shot back. "Panicking will not help." She noted with interest that the morning shadows across the deck were starting to subtly shift.

Meanwhile Jedric continued to play the part of the harmless skipper. "You brought all these men just to guard one plane?"

Boyan was not so blasé. "Not just that, sir, no. There has been an attempt to sabotage highly-valued property of the Soviet People. I am here to impound your ship."

At that Jedric pulled up short, and Lilya and her companions with him. "I beg your pardon?" Jedric seemed to be in genuine shock. "Surely you don't think that little bit of damage was a credible sabotage effort?"

Boyan smiled his cat-with-a-canary-smile. "Not a serious one, no. But enough to justify unauthorized examinations of its internal workings, perhaps?"

"You can't be serious."

"Come now, Mr. Orianos. Surely even you, a foreign citizen, is aware that Inar would be very keen to get their hands on the *Forerunner?*"

"Are you suggesting there are agents of Inar aboard my ship?" Jedric's eyes flashed. "This is an outrage!"

"Your feelings on the matter are none of my concern." Boyan's voice brooked no argument. "Until I satisfy myself there is no further threat, your ship belongs to me." He turned to his assembled officers and snapped his fingers. "Comrade Sergeant Captain, disperse your men to their objectives and prepare the *Forerunner* for transport back to Moscow."

"Sir!"

Boyan turned next to Lilya. She was bewildered to see something akin to nostalgia in his eyes, and thought back to what Jedric had told her the night before.

But when Boyan spoke, it was not to her. "Mr. Orianos, I will see you in your cabin." His gaze drifted past Lilya's shoulder to Nilo. "As for this boy . . ."

"Boy?" Nilo began, but Lilya shushed him.

"Nilo, no. You can't fight this."

"But Lilya—"

Boyan went on as if he hadn't heard them. "The boy you will secure in his stateroom."

The door to the cabin flew open and two large officers helped Nilo into the room. By 'helped', of course, it is meant they shoved him in like he was a *pulkka* rider heading down a mountain slope. He stumbled forward and nearly landed in Costan's lap, who merely stared out the vacant windows.

"... *Boyan* ..."

Nilo got back to his feet and paced the room as the door slammed behind him. He plucked at his jacket as if he didn't know what to do with his hands, then rubbed his face, scratched his head, and finally sank to the floor in despair.

Jedric's cabin was an austere space finished in polished metal and pale goatskin leather. Jedric sat in an understated Bergère chair as Boyan paced before him in a relaxed manner, like a schoolmaster lecturing an errant student.

"You mentioned the possibility of an Inar agent aboard your ship," the deputy was saying.

"I believe," Jedric corrected him, "that it was *you* that made that suggestion."

Boyan stopped his pacing and loomed over the medium. "We can dispute whose idea it was, but in any case, I do believe there are subversives at work here."

"Do you?" Jedric leaned back, crossed one leg over the other, and clasped his knee. "What led you to that conclusion?"

Boyan made his way to Jedric's desk and began idly thumbing the papers there, disturbing their neat arrangement, then putting them back in place with meticulous precision. "Persons of interest have been leaving the country, and many of their trails lead here." He turned back to Jedric, face smug. "And end here."

"Indeed? And from thence?"

"Does that truly matter?" He helped himself to the brandy. "They don't come back. Therefore, someone is facilitating their escapes. Someone known as . . ." Boyan stepped up close and leaned into Jedric's face. "'The Conductor.'"

Jedric stared up into Boyan's heavy-lidded eyes and smiled. "'The Conductor'? How provocative! It sounds like something right out of a pulp fiction novel!"

Boyan stood up and stepped back, apparently irked at Jedric's benign response. "I wonder how you do it, this theater of yours? Smoke and mirrors? Hallucinogenics?" He leaned on the windowsill and regarded Jedric as one would an old friend. "Would you care to know what I think?"

"Do tell."

"I think *you* are an agent of The Conductor."

Jedric laughed heartily. "I think I am going to enjoy this. Go on, enlighten me," he encouraged.

"You have a luxury ship that crosses borders with impunity. A large crew into which fugitives may fade easily."

"Wouldn't a gaggle of frightened refugees give themselves away?"

"A very good point and one I cannot as yet explain. But I have a feeling once I begin searching, I will find my answers."

"Have a care, Deputy. It's easy to find things one is convinced are there." He winked conspiratorially at the agent. "I should know."

"Sarcasm does not become one of your caliber, *Agent* Orianos." His voice took on a much more businesslike tone. "The Conductor is aboard this ship."

The *Spirit Walker* had been as quiet as doom since the engines had been shut down and she had been left to drift, and the silence in the cabin was getting on Nilo's already frayed nerves.

He kicked an occasional table over in frustration. Costan started and began trembling, and instantly Nilo felt ashamed of himself for frightening the old man. He thought about the bottle of akvavit but decided against it, not having Jedric around to tell him how much was enough without being too much. The last thing he needed was a drunken zombie stumbling around and crashing into things. Completely at a loss, he stood his father up and began walking him around the room in the hopes of tiring him out, or taking his mind off whatever was plaguing him, or something.

The door opened and a waitress was let in by the officer standing outside. She was carrying a tray laden with bread and water.

"Where do you want this, sir?" Her question was directed to Costan, and she seemed puzzled when he didn't answer.

"Umm . . . Just here is fine," Nilo replied, leaving his father to stand the table back up. He watched the waitress as she placed the tray down, and realized he recognized her from the dining salon when he and Lilya had been on their way to the sessorium. There was still something else nagging him about her . . . some recollection of her beyond the previous night. He struggled to bring the impression to light, and tried to get a good look at her face as she stood back up and turned for the door.

"Hey! Miss—"

She looked quickly back. Her pale blue eyes were skittish, and when her hand jumped to her face and her fingers drummed along her jaw the image in his mind leaped into sharp clarity: a gray smock, a white apron, and a short veil topped by a white canister-shaped coif marked with a red cross.

"You—you're Nurse Tatanya! From the hospital!" He paused, suddenly uncertain when she looked confused. "Aren't you?"

To his chagrin her expression became suddenly wary. "I'm sorry, sir? You must have me confused with someone else."

"No, you were . . . um . . ." Nilo fumbled. "I'm sure of it." But he wasn't, not now anyway. "I don't suppose you have a sister?" he finished lamely.

The waitress took a step back, her face a mask of apprehensive innocence. "Will there be anything else, sir?" Her tone implied she was sincerely hoping there wasn't.

"No . . . I suppose not . . . . No, thank you."

The waitress turned and rapped on the door. The officer let her out, and Nilo was left alone with Costan, and his doubts.

Mostly about what the waitress had said.

He stared at the closed door, then turned and laid out what was apparently all there was going to be for dinner. May as well get used to this, he thought. Bread and water. Standard prison fare. Once he was done, he gripped the serving tray until his knuckles were white. Something was afoot, but he didn't know what, and he didn't know how to find out. And Lilya was gone . . . He flung the tray against the wall.

The covering tore and the tray disappeared out of sight.

Nilo stopped in amazement, then crossed to the tear and peeked through.

"'All the bulkheads are fabric, young sir, for lightness,'" he repeated. As he looked into the dark abyss beyond the curtain a perilous thought rose above the bubbling fear in his mind. Maybe things weren't so hopeless after all. But he was alone—Lilya was on the hangar deck, Armas was as well, his father was still locked in his own head, and who knew what game Jedric was playing? He thought back to the old man on the train. One shouldn't play, he had said, if you can't watch all the pieces.

He looked back at Costan, pulled the scrap of newspaper from his pocket, and his mouth curled down into a frown. Where had this paper come from? Had his father really written the plea for help? Had he known what was happening, as it was happening? Did he leave this for his children to find?

"Boyan did this to us." That much he knew.

But now he needed more information. He needed to find out what all the pieces were doing, right now.

He needed to know, and there was no one else who could find out. And when he did—

"Then Boyan will undo it." He ripped the opening wide and stepped through.

<h1 style="text-align:center">XIII</h1>

NILO SLIPPED along the maintenance catwalks, not certain where he was going or for what he was looking, or even how he would know when he'd found it, but he was definitely certain that sooner or later, someone would pay.

He ignored the empty dining salon as he passed over it. Beyond that was the galley, identified by glimpses through ventilation grates and access hatches of stainless steel counters and implements. Then there were more serviceable rooms that he took to be crew quarters, then a mess hall, then a smaller dining area (the word 'wardroom' came to mind from some book he had read once), and finally small individual cabins grouped around the main passageway.

Officer country, he thought.

He heard voices. Up until now most of the ship had been quiet as the souls aboard dealt with their new circumstances as prisoners of the Soviet State. But on the faint wisps of air moving through the cavernous interior of the *Spirit Walker* he caught the smooth tones of Jedric, interlaced with the terse, precise enunciation of Deputy Boyan.

Boyan! Suddenly Nilo felt he knew why his father had been compelled to repeat *that* name, even if he could manage nothing else.

He crept toward the source of the sound, another cloth-walled chamber glowing from within like the sessorium. He leaned in close to an air vent.

"So, you encouraged the Lieutenant to come here so your sabotage would justify impounding my ship?" the medium was saying.

"Old tricks are the best tricks, no?" was Boyan's smug reply.

This sounded, Nilo thought, like it was just what he was in search of.

"Well, Deputy Boyan, you are indeed too clever for me. As a matter of fact, . . . I *am* an agent."

Nilo gasped and nearly slipped off the catwalk. He may have missed the first part of their conversation, but it was pretty clear where it was going and he wasn't about to miss the rest. He recovered without making an excessive amount of noise and stretched around to look through the grate.

Boyan was drawing a pistol on Jedric.

"I thank you for not insulting me by trying to deny it any further," Boyan said with a hard edge in his voice. "Now I'm sure you will understand that I—"

"Working for Red Army Intelligence," Jedric finished in a self-satisfied tone of his own.

Boyan's gun wavered. "I beg your pardon?"

"Don't beg, Deputy. It's . . . how did you say? *Unbecoming of an agent of your caliber.*"

Unseen above them Nilo nodded, impressed.

The fake spiritualist was castling.

Back in the stateroom Costan shambled around the furniture, came to the tear in the wall Nilo had left, and shuffled through.

Boyan scowled but the gun remained trained on Jedric's chest. "You have credentials, I presume?"

"Would a badge suffice?"

"Badges can be faked."

"I have my personal wireless just there, behind that panel." Jedric nodded to a cabinet door over the desk. "You could make a call, if you wished."

"And who would I be calling?"

"General Sascha Imran, Army Group Twelve Headquarters, based outside Morograd."

Boyan studied Jedric narrowly, then crossed carefully to the cabinet and opened it to reveal a military-grade radio.

Without lowering his weapon, he flipped switches and picked up the handset.

"Hello?" he said into the microphone after a moment's pause. "This is Deputy Ion Boyan of the Secret Police. Connect me to Army Group Twelve HQ. I need to speak to General Imran. It is a matter of the utmost import."

Miles away in a squat brick building just outside Morograd the gray-templed and lanky General Imran was chewing on a cigar that most certainly had come from unauthorized sources and signing papers with a pompous flair. There was a respectful knock at his office door and his adjutant poked in his head.

Imran looked up and frowned. "Yes, Veselsky?"

"Call for you, Comrade General. Secret Police."

Imran rolled his eyes. "Agh! What do they want?"

"He didn't say, sir, only that it was very important."

"It's always 'very important.'" He mashed out the cigar on a cheap tin ashtray. "Very well. Put him through."

Veselsky eased the door shut and a moment later General Imran's phone started ringing. He poured himself a drink, re-lit the cigar, let it ring several more times, and only then picked up the receiver. "Imran here. How may I be of assistance?"

The earpiece crackled with Boyan's distant voice. "*Comrade General. Deputy Boyan, Director of Secret Police,*

Moroskaya sector. Tell me, Comrade General, are you familiar with Jedric Orianos, the spirit medium?"

Imran jerked the phone away and stared at it for a second before putting it to his ear again. "This is 'important'?" He shrugged to himself. "Very well. I am. Who isn't?"

"Is he one of your agents?"

"Is he—" Again he stared at the receiver, but this time with a more suspicious look. "Why would you ask me such a thing?"

"It is important to our national security, Comrade General."

"And what would lead me to believe you could be trusted with that information?"

"Do not toy with me, Comrade General. I can make even simple things very difficult for you."

"Pah. Simple things are always the most difficult anyway. Is this a secure connection? You still haven't told me why you need to know this."

He could almost hear the man on the other end of the line twisting his face in frustration. *"On second thought, Comrade General, never mind. You have as much as answered me anyway."*

Boyan slammed the handset down on the desk and stared at Jedric through slitted eyes. "This changes nothing, you know."

Jedric, though, only got up and opened a bottle of mineral water. "We appear to be at a stand-off. Oh, don't look so glum, Deputy, you did gain *something* out of this. At least now you know *I'm* not The Conductor, yes?" He took a sip and smacked his lips. "I'm truly sorry that didn't work out for you. Care for another drink?"

Meanwhile, in the shadows above the cabin, Nilo struck off into the skeleton of the airship.

Time for a knight to block a rook.

On the hangar deck Armas finished up his repairs and helped the Apostolov technicians pack up their tools. Lilya watched from a short distance away, as several officers watched her.

As they lined up for inspection one of the guardsmen waved his Korovin service pistol at the group. "Empty your pockets." He turned to Lilya. "You too, Lieutenant."

Lilya's brow arched at the affront. "Anything you say, *Comrade.*" She patted her coveralls down, realized she was still carrying Costan's wallet, and dropped it on the workbench.

The officer began pawing through the group's assorted tools and belongings. He flipped open the wallet, saw only the folded handbill, and handed the wallet back to Lilya seemingly absently, though there was a subtle, apologetic look toward her that he was clearly keeping from his superiors. Lilya almost did a double-take, but recovered before she could give him away. She took the wallet in hand and turned to look in another direction, rubbing the back of her neck with her free hand.

There, on the far side of the *Forerunner*, she spotted Costan shuffling his aimless way along the deck. Members of the *Spirit Walker*'s crew were staring in confusion and Secret Police officers were moving to intercept him.

"You had one task, Nilo," she grumbled under her breath and dashed around the plane. She took him by the hand and turned him around so she was standing between him and the approaching officers. "Father, come along." She tried to coax him away from the aircraft but he stumbled and fell to his knees, and when she tried to catch him, she dropped the wallet.

The leather flopped open. She watched fearfully as the lockpicking tools splayed out across the deck plates, but she froze when she saw the pressed lily waft out of the creased handbill . . .

Ruddy gaslight reflected in driving rain outside the window. Costan, every inch a argent-templed aristocrat in boutonniere-and-bowtie, stood gloomily at his desk in his study and regarded the storm.

She was standing in the doorway in an evening gown, hair artfully pinned back under a tiara made of fresh lilies.

"Papa! . . . Papa?" Her voice was pleading. It was the last time it would be so.

Costan looked at that floor, she assumed too ashamed to face her.

Lilya's voice broke. "You don't talk to us anymore. It's like we don't even exist! You lost mom, well . . . we did too! How can you treat us like this?"

She hurled the tiara onto his desk, as if to force some part of her into his field of view to make him acknowledge her presence. But he only sank heavily into his chair and said nothing.

"I won't live this way anymore!" she cried. "I just won't!" She stormed out the door, and the last thing she saw as she turned to slam it shut was her father picking the tiara off the desk, crushing it in his hand . . .

Lilya looked up from the flower and, as luck would have it, right to the lily emblem she herself had painted on the nose of the *Forerunner*. She looked back down at the flower again, fragile and tiny on the cold metal expanse of the deck.

She cradled it tenderly in her hand, marveled at its preserved delicacy, and pondered what its presence in her father's wallet meant. He had always been so strong. He could do anything, which meant if he *didn't* do something, it was because he didn't want to. This one fact had been the driving force behind her life for the last two years, pushing her to join the army, to qualify as a pilot, to rise through ranks and prestige and become who she was. She had never wanted to admit it, but deep within herself she knew his indifference after her mother's death had been a large part of how *she* had become what she now was.

But if all that hadn't mattered to him, why was this lily here? She could still see the threads that had secured it to her tiara. Could it be that something of what she and her father had shared in bygone years had meant enough to him to inspire him to preserve this frail memento?

There was a silvery glint in her hand under the yellowed petals. Her mother's ring. She looked to her father's left hand, where his own wedding band yet endured.

He hadn't talked that night, and now he wasn't speaking at all. Was it, as she had told Nilo during the drive back from the hospital, another rung on a ladder started down long ago, as she had accused? But not one of his choosing, as she had assumed? Was it not that he wouldn't speak, but that he couldn't? Had he found himself in over his head and *hadn't* known what to do next?

Much as she herself was feeling now, here with Secret Police all around?

Could it be he was really just someone who had been deprived of someone close to him, and could do nothing more than to try to keep close a lingering fragment of each soul he had lost?

She looked again at her mother's ring on her hand, and her vision blurred and her throat tightened.

Shadows clustered around her as the officers moved in to collect Costan and she waved them off. "I'm sorry," she choked. "I don't know how he got out." She folded the flower into the handbill, tucked them into her pocket, and took her father by the hand. "Come along. Come along . . . Papa."

Armas finally was able to squeeze between the officers to help her. He appeared completely flummoxed at her state. "You . . . all right?" he managed.

Lilya nodded and rubbed her eyes with the heels of her hands. "I am. I just . . . I just realized something."

One of the officers stooped to collect Costan's tools from the deck. "Hey . . ."

Nilo slipped out the access door onto the flight deck and scrambled on his hands and knees against the slipstream. Though the *Spirit Walker* was only drifting, there was still a stiff wind over the open space that was hard to push against. Put that together with the Secret Police craft scattered all over the deck and their attendant stewards to be avoided, and Nilo had his work cut out for him.

He scanned around from behind the fat main tire of a gaudily-marked Airspeed Envoy.

There. Boyan's plane. He scampered for what cover he could find until he could crawl under the low-slung wing and inspect what was securing the tie-downs.

The plane was fastened to the deck with thick chains closed with combination locks. Normally this wouldn't be a problem for Nilo; listening for the tumblers to fall was easy enough, if one was careful.

But it couldn't be done with drafts gusting in one's ears.

He had indeed assumed the planes would be locked down. He had *hoped* his skills would enable him to jam those locks so they could not be opened and keep Boyan from running, now that Jedric was turning the tables on him. It had become clear the *Spirit Walker*'s master had something up his sleeve and Nilo wanted the chance to watch the proceedings in the hopes of somehow finding an angle that could be used to get the Deputy to revoke Lilya's mission.

Or at least give him the opportunity to exact a little revenge.

But combination locks . . . that was not going to work here. He plopped down on the deck, not sure what to do next.

There was a commotion on the far side of the plane. He edged around the tail to get a look at the junior officers and ducked back quickly when he saw them looking his way. But when he realized they were looking *over* his head at something beyond him, his throat closed up with dread.

There wasn't much that could reach them up here. Not that would make *them* afraid.

He turned slowly, and nearly fell back against the plane's rudder when he saw it. Surely, he could touch it with his hand as it skimmed overhead if he only reached out—

"These look like lockpicks!" the officer exclaimed. He scooped them up and held them out to Armas. "What are you doing with lockpicks?"

"Oh, no," Armas chuckled, just a little nervously. "They're for fine cleaning of parts. Here, like this." He took the tools, selected one with some thought, and plucked a small hydraulic valve off the workbench.

Suddenly a blaring klaxon horn echoed overhead. The hangar deck windows went dark as something immense swung over the *Spirit Walker* and settled along its sunward side.

A thunderous voice, seemingly from the gods themselves, washed over Lilya, Armas, Costan, and the assembled officers and technicians, all now together frozen in dread.

"Attention. Attention. Passengers and crew of the Spirit Walker. *This is Air Destroyer* Dogoda. *You have entered controlled airspace without authorization. Prepare to be boarded."*

In the glare of the sun, Lilya made out another airship coming to alongside the *Spirit Walker*. Three, in fact. One smaller than Jedric's craft, though still large, and two small frigate-class zeppelins. All were emblazoned with bold red stars, and all were bristling with gun turrets on revolving mounts.

All of which were trained on the *Spirit Walker*.

XIV

THE *DOGODA* dropped ballast, rose up, and took a position directly over the *Spirit Walker*. Long ropes dangled from its belly, down which squads of Naval Infantry rappelled, then heavy mooring cables were lowered, to be gathered up by the infantry to secure the two ships together.

The soldiers then spread out over the flight deck and poured down every available companionway and elevator into the lower levels. They erupted from service doors and rapidly dispersed into small squads, covering stunned crew, passengers, and Secret Police officers alike with compact and deadly machine pistols.

Nilo poked his head out from where he had taken up hiding behind the sessorium and watched the green-clad troops dominate the ship inside and out. Thinking better of his overall situation, he decided to head back up.

His only hope now was that Lilya probably would know what to do and have some kind of authority to do it.

Jedric swept onto the *Spirit Walker*'s bridge, Boyan hard on his heels. Ursula turned to face him but as she opened her mouth to give report, she froze, looking over her captain's shoulder. Jedric turned.

An infantry lieutenant stood in the doorway flanked by a squad of troops.

"Sir?" the young man asked. "Are you the master of this vessel?"

"I am," Jedric replied calmly.

Boyan stepped in front of the medium. "*I* am in charge here."

The lieutenant didn't bat an eye. "Very good. Would both of you please come with me to the flight deck? Admiral Bryndas wants to see you."

The flight deck was crowded with people. Civilians, crew, hospitality staff, and Secret Police officers had all been brought up into the biting airstream and sorted into groups by the soldiers. Jedric gave his people reassuring nods as he was led past, but Boyan's expression could have curdled goat's milk.

That was small comfort for Nilo, corralled by the soldiers on his way topside and now standing with Lilya, Armas, and Costan among the civilian patrons.

The lieutenant led Jedric and Boyan to a stop at a large area that had been left clear of detainees. All eyes looked up at a rumbling whir overhead where a large crate-like pod was swaying in the wind as it was winched down.

It settled on the deck with a thump that seemed to echo far under the deck. A squad of soldiers locked it down and opened a large hatchway, and a stocky woman in her sixties, uniform glittering with gold braid and medals, stepped out with a gaunt captain with a pinched face close on her heels.

Admiral Gertrude Bryndas, Commander Soviet Navy Airborne Forces, glared down her wide nose at the shivering crowds arrayed before her.

The infantry lieutenant snapped to attention and saluted. "Comrade Admiral!"

Bryndas returned the salute with the practiced precision of a career officer and immediately turned to the lieutenant's two charges.

"Which one of you is Orianos?"

Jedric took a step forward. "I am, Comrade Admiral. Very pleased to meet you."

Once again Boyan stepped to the fore. "I am Deputy Ion Boyan of the Secret Police. What is the meaning of this?"

Bryndas looked down her nose at Boyan like she was trying to figure out what the dog had brought in from the woods. "The meaning of this, Deputy, is that I am taking charge of this vessel."

"Indeed? By what authority do you claim control?"

Bryndas' next words were to her scarecrow-like companion. "Captain Kinsky?"

"This vessel," he recited in the voice Nilo recognized from the booming loudspeakers of the *Dogoda*, "has made an unauthorized incursion into controlled airspace."

Bryndas looked at Boyan with one eyebrow raised. "Just so." She scanned the shivering, motley assembly of prisoners ranged before her. "Whatever kind of party you've had going on here is over. This is now a military matter." She made a point of turning away from Boyan and addressed Jedric directly. "Mr. Orianos, can you explain your presence here?"

"I will certainly endeavor to, Comrade Admiral. If I may?" He slowly lifted the lapel of his jacket to show the pocket within. When she nodded her permission, he reached in, removed a small wallet and opened it to reveal an ornate badge. "I am with Red Army Intelligence, working undercover aboard this ship for Army Group Twelve under General Imran."

"General Imran?" Bryndas' tone became unexpectedly soft as she took the badge and examined it carefully, but she quickly dropped a professional mask over her features as she handed it to Kinsky, who studied it as well.

Among the ranks of civilians, Nilo saw Lilya's jaw drop. "I was coming to tell you," he whispered, but the naval infantry guardsmen half-blocking their view turned to glare at him, and he shut up.

Kinsky handed the badge back. Bryndas ignored the glare Boyan was turning on her. "And your friend here?"

"Yes, Comrade Admiral. Deputy Boyan. He had arranged a pretext for the *Forerunner* to land here carrying a small explosive device—"

Once again Lilya's mouth fell open, but Nilo, watching the stiff shoulders of the guard in front of him, said nothing.

Bryndas cut Jedric off. "The *Forerunner*? You mean the research aircraft?"

"Yes, Comrade Admiral." Jedric barreled on, exuding confidence. "When the device discharged the Deputy used the damage to justify boarding us."

Bryndas finally turned to acknowledge Boyan. "Is this true, Deputy?"

Boyan hesitated only long enough to signal his displeasure. "So far as it goes," was his aloof reply.

"Of course," Jedric continued, "it was only a ploy to board us with enough force to take control of my ship."

"To what end?"

"He is a defector seeking asylum in Inar Province. He was looking for someone called 'The Conductor'."

Boyan's eyes flashed. "That is ludicrous!"

Bryndas held up a hand to him. "Please hold your comments until I get to you, Deputy."

Now it was Nilo's turn to be surprised. "That's not what he said in Jedric's cabin . . ." But the guard was giving him another evil look.

Jedric took a breath and carried on. "When this 'Conductor' failed to appear he instead offered me the *Forerunner* to buy passage out of Moroskaya. I believe he was feeling some desperation."

Boyan apparently could contain himself no longer. "This is preposterous. Comrade Admiral, I protest! How can you find any of this believable—"

"It's too early," Bryndas cut him off with a stern tone, "to know precisely what I *should* believe. At this point I'm still trying to figure out why this ship is even here."

Jedric's mouth curled up into an apologetic twist. "I am afraid that was my doing, Comrade Admiral. As the deputy took control, I sent the distress signal and ordered a course change to bring us here."

"Did you? Then I am your strong arm?"

"I'm sorry, Comrade Admiral, but yes. I felt I would be in need of support."

"Comrade Admiral, I insist—"

"For the last time, Deputy, shut it!"

Nilo, for his part, was amazed. He had heard about the rivalry between the military and the Secret Police, but to see it now, firsthand . . . if anyone else had even *dared* to speak so to an officer of the Secret Police, let alone a Deputy, the result would have been catastrophic.

"Agent Orianos," Bryndas went on, "your crew is Merchant Marine, are they not?"

"They are, ma'am."

"Then by maritime law I am placing them under my direct control. Until I sort this out, they will answer only to me. Do you understand?"

"Yes, Comrade Admiral." Jedric's demeanor was every bit the dutiful subordinate.

"Furthermore, you will be confined to your cabin and are to have no direct contact with the crew unless I permit it. Deputy!"

"Comrade Admiral?" Boyan's voice dripped with ice.

"Your men will stand down and turn in their weapons. Assemble them in my pod at once."

"I will do no such thing, Comrade Admiral. I do not answer to the Navy."

"Oh? We are over the water, sir. Shall I quote maritime law for you? Or shall I phone the Secretary-General himself? I can, if you would like."

Boyan's fists balled up in his jacket sleeves but his face was rigidly impassive. "I am sure, Comrade Admiral, that will not be necessary." He stepped away without another word to address his penned officers.

Bryndas gave him an indignant look at the rebuff but managed to not roll her eyes as she turned back to Jedric. "Agent Orianos."

Jedric snapped his attention back from watching Boyan himself. "Comrade Admiral?"

"You may direct your crew to see to the disposition of your passengers. We should get them off this deck right away."

Jedric snapped his heels together and bowed. "At once, ma'am." He waved to Perun to carry out the order.

"And one other thing?" Bryndas continued.

"Ma'am?"

"Where is the *Forerunner*?"

"The Deputy has it locked down on the hangar deck below us."

"Kinsky, have the plane brought up for transfer to the *Dogoda*. Whatever else happens we'll be taking it back with us. Where is the pilot?"

Lilya stepped forward. "Here, Comrade Admiral."

Bryndas looked her over with a calculating eye. "Lieutenant, collect your gear and report here at my pod in twenty minutes for transfer to the *Dogoda*. Counterintelligence will want a word with you."

There was a clear and, to Nilo, frightening tremor in Lilya's voice as she answered, "Y—yes, Comrade Admiral."

By the time the massed civilians, crew, police, and soldiers had been sent their various ways and the elevator doors were finally closing on Nilo and his family, the *Forerunner* was rising on the deck lift into the sunlight.

XV

COSTAN STARED blankly out the stateroom windows as clouds built dramatically in the distance. The late afternoon sun picked out their majestic shapes in brilliant detail, and Lilya thought the sight would have been breathtaking, if she had been in a mood to appreciate it.

The only things marring the sight were the thick mooring cables just beyond the glass, a stark reminder of the *Spirit Walker*'s imprisonment.

Lilya stared out the window also, nearly as blankly as her father, with her kit beside her on the floor and clenching her flight jacket in her fists. Nilo paced restlessly while Armas simply stood in the middle of the room and hugged himself.

"Why did Lenin wear shoes, but Stalin wears boots?" the engineer began, more or less to himself. "Because in Lenin's time we were only ankle deep in—Nilo, can you stop?"

"How?" Nilo fretted, spreading his hands. "Jedric's screwed up everything, getting Boyan taken by the Navy!"

"How so? I would think you'd want the guy gone."

"But Papa's in this . . . this . . ." he sputtered in frustration. "Because of him! How are we going to get him to revoke Lilya's mission now? Because if he doesn't, we'll probably never be able to make Papa better!" He smacked his fist into his open palm.

Lilya plucked at her jacket, and her voice was small. "No point in that in any case."

"Why not?" Nilo demanded.

"I couldn't understand why he helped us at the checkpoint, but now I do." She looked around at each of them. "We were his pawns."

"Well, he's about to get his," Nilo asserted bitterly. "There's a great big queen in an admiral's uniform got him squarely in her sights."

Lilya shook her head. "You don't understand. Bryndas is going to interrogate me because she thinks we colluded with Boyan."

"What's the difference?" Nilo's frustration showed. "You were convinced we were going to be arrested anyway."

"Yes. By the Police. But my rank would have helped, at least a little, and the army would have intervened on our behalf. You saw how she talked to him. But now?" She sighed and turned her eyes back out over the distant waters of the Inar Gulf. "Now we're going to be taken by the military themselves. Now there's no one to protect us."

She yanked the epaulets off her jacket. "Whatever happens to me, *you* will go to the gulag for this. And it is my fault for bringing you here."

"Your fault? You told Jedric it was my idea."

"I know I did. The idea was yours originally. But it *is* my fault. *I* decided to go along with it. I suppose deep down inside I hoped you would find a way to fix him." Her eyes trailed off to Costan, standing oblivious to the entire exchange.

"All right, so? So it was both our doing."

"But you wanted it, to make him better. I only wanted it . . . I only wanted to make him apologize."

Nilo looked at Armas with a question in his eyes, but the engineer only shrugged helplessly.

"But I'm the one that needs to tell him I'm sorry," Lilya finished. "And now I won't ever be able to."

She opened the window and pitched her epaulets into the void beyond.

Nilo jumped up, mouth agape. "Lilya! Why did you do that?"

"I wanted him to beg me to forgive him!" Her voice was getting shrill but she could not bring herself to stop. It all had to come out, once and for all. "So I could ignore him!"

"But you worked hard for that rank!"

"Yes! I worked hard for *me* to have that rank! Just to show *him.* Just to throw it in his face. Just to hurt him!" She sank heavily into a chair and buried her face in her hands. "But in the end, it was just a badge. It was nothing useful. At least *he* made people happy. Made people surprised. Made them marvel. What did *I* do? Was I useful? No. Just like that badge. Just nothing."

Nilo looked again at Armas, who by now was looking at the younger man suggestively. A look came over Nilo's face, like he was just beginning to understand, and he stepped quietly past his sister to close the window. Then he reached down and gently pried the jacket from Lilya's hands.

"You . . . you're not nothing." He took a deep breath as if he were stepping into uncharted territory. "Papa brags about you a lot." He pulled out the wallet, withdrew the handbill, and unfolded it. With great care he lifted the pressed lily free and laid it on the armrest beside his sister.

He then plucked the Air Force Excellency badge off his own jacket. "And to be honest . . . I have too, at times." He dropped the badge on the chair next to the flower, took another breath, and drew himself up to his full height.

"Lilya Costanevna Campalia. You're right, you brought us here. We wouldn't have gotten here without you. And we wouldn't have learned as much as we had about what happened to Papa, and we wouldn't have had a hope of healing him if you hadn't. At least now we know what we're up against. Now, maybe, we have a chance. I don't know how, just yet, but we might . . . . Yes, you brought us here. But we won't get out without you, either. So you're not nothing . . . not by half."

Lilya didn't look up, but her hand reached out to touch the flower, and then the badge, and her shoulders began to shake.

The pod winched back up into the *Dogoda*'s underside bay and locked into place. The hatchway opened and Bryndas exited with Kinsky, closely followed by Boyan.

Boyan stopped on the deck's main catwalk. "Comrade Admiral, a word?"

Bryndas stopped, considered, and nodded to Kinsky. "Take the bridge. I will be along shortly."

"Yes, Comrade Admiral." Kinsky snapped off a hurried salute and headed forward.

Bryndas motioned Boyan off to a small maintenance office a few yards away. Inside she pointed to a seat, but Boyan remained standing. She did as well, though the deck began pitching as the wind began to rise.

She got straight to the point. "What's on your mind, Deputy?"

"I must return to the *Spirit Walker*. You have disrupted my investigation of human trafficking there."

Bryndas noted he made no mention of being *permitted* to do so. She decided on a different tack. "Did your investigation include turning one of your own men into a vegetable? That was *your* man down there, was it not?"

Boyan brushed off her recrimination. "An unexpected turn. Our initial plan was simply to have the Lieutenant deliver a small package."

"You mean a bomb. *That* was your original plan? Then how did your man come to be in his current state?"

"Agent Campalia was convinced the Air Force would not allow us to make use of the *Forerunner*."

"And so, he went aboard to spy instead. And came back as he is now?"

"Yes, quite. I have not yet determined exactly how that has happened, though rest assured, Comrade Admiral, in time I shall."

"Especially if more charges can be brought as a result of your findings," she added drily.

Boyan glowered at her. "It was after his return that I decided to revert to our original plan."

"You weren't concerned with the Air Force's opinion then?"

"The situation *had* escalated, Comrade Admiral."

"Yet either way you decided to set a very expensive and experimental aircraft as bait. With a bomb!"

Boyan drew himself up indignantly. "Comrade Admiral, I will have you know the Secret Police have had charge of the *Forerunner*'s security since the beginning. The ship was never in any real danger. The device was essentially harmless though, I might point out, very effective."

"At least until this afternoon. Tell me, Deputy. Was it worth it? Did you at least find what you were seeking?"

"I had only just confronted Orianos about the presence of The Conductor when you arrived." Now Boyan's tone was laden with his own recriminations. "So, no."

Bryndas nodded knowingly. "Yes. This 'Conductor'. A mysterious figure helping people leave the country without authorization. That would have been quite a feather in your cap. How lamentable that I arrived."

"Comrade Admiral," Boyan's voice had a sharp edge. "There are yet subversives aboard that ship. I cannot allow this interference. The Secret Police—"

"The Secret Police are not in charge here, Deputy! How many times am I going to have to remind you of that fact? Have you no appreciation of your situation here?"

If anything, Bryndas' rebuke angered Boyan even further. "Comrade Admiral! I care little for your relationship, professional or otherwise, with General 'Immie'! Or—" he raised a hand to stifle her retort, "even if you dine at the Secretary-General's own table! I will not be sidelined by conniving, toad-strangling elites! I can see now why the *kulaks* are fleeing the country!"

"That will do, Deputy!" Bryndas stepped up nose to nose with Boyan and punctuated her rebuke with hard jabs of her finger into his chest. "*You* recklessly endangered a priceless aircraft that belongs to 'The People' *you* profess to be so eager to serve. *You* lost track of one of your own men to the point of him being left completely mindless, and *you* endangered several hundred people aboard what is still, as far as *I* know, only a foreign civilian vessel—"

The intercom buzzed impatiently. Bryndas stopped in mid-tirade and slammed the switch. "What is it?"

Kinsky's voice echoed from the speaker. "*Ma'am, the wind's picking up. I don't think we can get the* Forerunner *transferred safely.*"

"Very well. Leave it where it is and instruct the *Spirit Walker* to follow us to the shipyard."

"*Will do, ma'am. And, ma'am? Orianos is asking to release his guests before the weather worsens.*"

Boyan shook his head but Bryndas gave him an irritated glare and turned back to the speaker. "Tell him to go ahead."

"*Yes, Comrade Admiral. By your command.*"

Boyan leaned back against the bulkhead and crossed his arms. "You've made a grave mistake."

Bryndas turned for the door. "You can have the manifest if you want, Deputy, and you can track down your suspects later. But if any of that flock of starlets and nabobs are spies, like you say, I don't want any of them in my shipyard."

"I must get back down there. Now."

"You will stay right here."

"Comrade Admiral—"

"*My ship, Deputy,*" she hissed dangerously. "My rules. Don't think I won't have you thrown off the launch deck if I feel the need." She stepped out and slammed the door behind her.

Boyan fumed and looked out a porthole to the *Spirit Walker* a hundred feet below. "Yes," he whispered to himself. "Now I see how it is."

He waited long enough for Bryndas to be well on her way forward, then opened the door, checked the passageway, and slipped out.

XVI

LILYA CHECKED her watch and stood. "It's time." Her voice was heavy as she shouldered her pack and gave Nilo a half-smile. "Wish me—"

Ursula's voice crackled over the loudspeakers. "*Attention all passengers. Attention all passengers. Civilians have been cleared for departure. Report to your aircraft for immediate launch.*"

The message repeated as Nilo, Armas, and Lilya exchanged worried looks.

Nilo spoke first. "What is Jedric up to?"

Armas almost couldn't help himself. "I'd say just short of two meters?"

But Nilo was carrying on as if he hadn't heard. "He got the Secret Police *and* the Navy off his ship in one shot with that fake story about Boyan defecting—"

"Which was pretty weak, when you think of it."

"And now he's clearing off the passengers . . .what's he trying?"

The sound of doors slamming and anxious voices echoed in the passageway outside.

Armas gulped loudly as the sounds faded and the ship became as silent as a tomb. "And what kind of ride are we along for?"

Hundreds of feet away in his own cabin Jedric watched the clouds build and lightning flashed deep in their angry bellies. Closer in, surrounding the *Spirit Walker,* multicolored specks marked the escape of frightened civilians who had come for a thrill and had wound up with much more than they had bargained for.

He counted them as they set their courses for safer havens. Twenty-three . . . twenty-four . . . twenty-five . . . . He turned to his locker, tossed a flight jacket over his dinner attire, and flipped on his intercom.

"Bridge. Charges set?"

Ursula was terse. "*Charges are set, sir.*"

"Blow those mooring lines."

"*Aye, sir. Consider it done.*"

A loud rumble echoed through the ship, and beyond the cabin windows the thick cables began to drop.

The tremor shuddered through the frame of the *Spirit Walker* like a whale shaking itself awake.

Lilya looked up, eyes wide. "What was that?"

Nilo, on the other hand, was pressing his face against the window. "The cables! They've been cut!"

There was a sudden thrum, different this time, and Lilya and Nilo both looked to Armas for an explanation.

"It's the engines!" he replied as the deck lurched. He craned his neck toward the windows with a mixture of fear and relief as the navy ships fell away aft. "We're getting under way!"

"He's making a break for it!" Nilo exclaimed and slapped his forehead. "That's it! *He's* The Conductor! He must be running for Inar!"

Lilya took only a heartbeat to process her brother's revelation. "Looks like we are as well." Her jaw set as she watched the navy ships grow smaller, too slowly. "Nilo. Armas. We need to get Papa out of here. Things are going to get hot very quickly."

Nilo was suddenly uncertain. "But our plane is gone!"

"Yes. But Boyan's is still up there."

"It's locked down! With combination locks!"

"Then we will just have to find bolt cutters on our way up through the hangar deck. Let's go. Now!"

Nilo dashed to the torn flap of bulkhead, passed through, and then reached back for Costan.

Armas handed off the old man and paused for just a moment before following. He turned back to Lilya. "Good to have you back, ma'am."

Lilya shook her head. "Not back, Armas. But certainly, in a different place. But thank you. Now go—with a quickness!"

Bryndas barged into the bridge of the *Dogoda* with a look that could have lit charcoal.

"Comrade Admiral!" Kinsky was breathless at the audacity of Jedric's move. "The *Spirit Walker* is breaking away!"

"I can see that!"

Kinsky stepped aside as she took her station at the helmsman's elbow. "He played us, ma'am." Kinsky's demeanor was almost embarrassed, and a little awe-struck. "Like a tin flute, he did."

"And now he's running." Bryndas, on the other hand, was consumed with indignation. "Helm! Full speed ahead. Fire control! Put a round across their bow! And I'm not too concerned," she added stiffly, "if you misjudge by a dozen yards."

The elevator reached the *Spirit Walker*'s flight deck and the door slid open. Lilya and Armas struggled to shield Costan as they guided him onto the deck. The wind was howling at gale force over the open expanse now that the airship was making real speed, and the thunderheads towering above were just beginning to let loose huge drops that soaked their skins in an instant.

Nilo dodged around them to show them the way to Boyan's transport when he skidded to a halt.

The *Forerunner* was still on the deck, lashed down to a cargo pallet.

"Look! It's still here!"

"We'll take it!" Lilya called. "It's a lot closer!"

"Going to be a tight fit!" Armas reminded her between gulps of air.

"I know. But we'll need the speed!"

The deck pitched and rolled under them and every few yards they had to stop to brace themselves so they wouldn't be thrown down. When they finally reached the comforting crimson flank of their craft Armas flung open the mail hatch and bodily lifted Costan inside. Lilya leaped up to the cockpit and slammed down into the pilot's seat as Nilo scrambled underneath with a pair of bolt cutters pilfered from the hangar deck below.

He half-ran, half-shuffled to the starboard wheel, but when he tried to fit the cutters over the hasp of the lock—

"It's too thick!"

He felt a stone drop in his stomach. He may not have known much about aviation, but everyone had heard about the American *USS Macon,* gone down a storm like this. Never mind the very angry trio of navy ships racing to catch them. And here was their only means of escape, locked down to what was going to be a death trap one way or another, and he had no way to get them loose.

A shadow loomed over him. He looked up.

It was Boyan.

"You!" Nilo raised the bolt cutters but had the quick sense to restrain himself. "You need to release my father! You need to revoke Lilya's mission!" Even as he spoke the words, they seemed pointless, given their inevitable fate.

For a long moment Boyan only stared at him. When he did speak, he was shouting, but only to be heard over the din of the gale. His voice, actually, was calm. "Whom do you choose, Nilo Campalia?"

Nilo could only stare back at him.

"Do you decide," Boyan went on, waving one hand as if offering up a plate of caviar, "to help an open defector that was once your friend?" He raised the other hand. "Or collude with smiling hypocrites that use rank and status for their own gain?

"How do you make an impossible choice?"

Nilo froze, uncertain what to say, but feeling with certainty Boyan already had his answer.

He was not disappointed.

"The answer, my boy, is to *change the question*." Boyan lifted the tie-down lock and thrust it into Nilo's hands. "Eleven, twenty-four, sixteen . . . the day I first met your parents."

Nilo dropped the bolt cutters and spun the tumblers. The lock popped open and Nilo looked up at Boyan, just as confused as he had been at the start. "Why—why are you letting us go?"

Boyan shook his head. "I'm not letting you go." He duck-walked back from under the wing, stood, and turned for his transport at the far end of the deck. Taking a moment to adjust his cuffs and tie in the blistering rain, he looked back at Nilo. "I'm washing my hands of you. *My* mission is complete. The Conductor is finished. But I'm not taking the fall for the *Forerunner*." He nodded with smug satisfaction toward the *Dogoda* and its flanking frigates and set off at a run.

Nilo watched him go, then shook himself and dashed out from under the wing.

Lilya let out a breath she hadn't realized she'd been holding when Nilo climbed up. She leaned to her intercom. "Clear!"

Armas started up the portside engine, but Nilo froze at the mail bay hatch.

Lilya saw him and leaned over the coaming. "Nilo! Get in!"

"Lilya, wait! I have to find Jedric!"

"What? Whatever for?"

"So we know who we can go to when we get to Inar!"

Before Lilya could stop him, he was off the wing and bolting for the elevators.

The windows of the *Spirit Walker*'s bridge rattled with the driving rain. Lightning flashed and a sudden unexpected beam of sunlight shone through as the lowering sun descended below the bellies of the clouds.

Ursula braced herself against the overhead framing as bright tracers streaked by a few dozen yards ahead of them.

The helmsman marked them as well. "Warning shots!"

"Steady, man," Ursula reassured him.

Jedric appeared in the hatchway. "Are the civilians away?"

"I believe they all are, sir. Sir?" Ursula's voice was calm. "The Reds have opened fire."

"Run out the guns. Return fire, smoke rounds. We need a screen."

Ursula nodded and slapped an alarm. She picked up the intercom mike as klaxon horns blared around the ship. "General quarters. General quarters. This is not a drill . . ."

Lilya struggled to keep the *Forerunner* from lifting into the air as the deck moved under them. Suddenly there was a shuddering boom that rivaled the building thunder, and smoke blossomed several hundred yards to their rear.

Armas' voice was panicky over the intercom. *"What was that? Are we hit?"*

Lilya shook her head at the realization of what had just happened. "He's returning fire. This thing is armed!"

"Armed!?" Armas' voice cracked with the tension. *"Is there anything on this gasbag that just is what it seems?"*

But Lilya only had eyes for the elevators. "Come on, Nilo, come *on*."

Jedric watched the *Dogoda* carefully. "What's that ship's maximum speed?"

"*Romani*-class destroyer, forty knots," Ursula recited. "Frigates a little faster."

Jedric's mouth cocked up in a lopsided grin. "Then we've a speed advantage. We'll do a Parthian Shot maneuver. Helm!"

"Aye, sir!"

"Make your course for Inar. Zig-zag pattern, alternate left and right standard rudder on a random timing. Flank speed. Keep us just out of their range."

"Zig-zag course for Inar at flank speed, aye, aye, sir."

Jedric grabbed the intercom mike. "Fire control."

"Fire control, aye."

"Load incendiary rounds. Alternate port and starboard batteries. Target the ships aft and fire at will."

"Incendiary rounds, firing at will, aye, aye, sir."

Along the flanks of the massive airship, ports opened and turrets of rocket tubes extended on racks. As the *Spirit Walker* tacked to the right the starboard tubes erupted in streaking flame. Rockets blasted rearward, punched through the building smoke screen, and struck the lead frigate in the nose.

In an instant the entire forward quarter of the pursuing ship detonated in a massive hydrogen explosion that knocked *Dogoda* askew. It began to fall, almost majestically, as tiny specks leaped from the gondola and blossomed into parachutes far below.

Bryndas picked herself back up from the deck as the *Dogoda*'s crew fought to right the ship.

"Admiral!" Kinsky called, forgetting his protocols. "The *Manifesto* is down!"

"Tell the *Mythos* to spread out. Load torpedoes. Flank speed! Get us through that smoke screen!"

Ursula watched the other frigate emerge from the wall of smoke the *Spirit Walker* had left behind. "They're dispersing and evading."

"Switch to flak rounds." Jedric did a double-take when he realized Nilo was standing in the door. "Nilo! Why are you still here?"

"It's you, isn't it?" There was something in the boy's voice, something that said, no matter what else, he *had* to know. He had to know what it had all been about.

"Nilo, we've engaged the enemy. I've no time for games. I'm what?"

"The Conductor," Nilo stated with the sure conviction of youth. "Army Intel was just a cover. You hypnotize people into a new identity so they won't give themselves away and you slip them out. You're a double agent!"

Shells burst nearby and shrapnel rattled the windows.

"How did you—but of course. Son of an escape artist. You snooped. I should have had you watched more closely."

"And you took us into navy airspace and maneuvered Bryndas to get Boyan off the ship." Nilo smirked appreciatively. "It's like an Arabian checkmate!"

"And I'm more relieved it worked than you can imagine!"

"Where are you going now?"

"Back home. Cover's blown."

"We want to go, too."

The helmsman spun the wheel and the deck tilted drunkenly.

"Really?"

"Boyan's gone. He can't revoke her mission. If we leave, get to where she *can't* take the mission, maybe that will be enough for Papa."

Jedric considered this and nodded. "Can you follow?"

More shells burst in the air nearby and Nilo flinched. "We have the *Forerunner*. But, begging your pardon, if you don't make it, who do we go to?"

Jedric had to hand it to him. For a kid, he was smart and motivated. "When you get to Inar tell the authorities you were part of Operation Charlatan. They'll handle it from there. Now get out of here! You have your clearance to leave!"

The *Dogoda* finally broke out of the smoke screen. A large tube nestled among its gun turrets belched fire and launched a missile the size of a rail car.

It streaked across the open sky separating it from the *Spirit Walker* and struck the larger vessel amidships. The detonation sent shock waves rippling across the fabric as the metal frame started to give way, and the clawing wind pushed into the internal structure and started prying the *Spirit Walker* in two.

One of the gas bags tore, venting helium, and the ship began to fall.

The impact shook the bridge harshly. The helmsman wrestled with his controls and quickly realized the danger. "We're hit! Losing speed—we can't maintain altitude!"

Jedric kept his voice steady to avoid panicking the crew. "Abandon ship. Sound the alarm. Ursula, call up our sub squadron, get them here now. We need fire support."

As Ursula hit the alarm again Jedric took Nilo by the shoulder. "Come with me, Nilo. We've got to get you out of here."

Ursula looked afraid, though her face seemed to have no real idea how to accomplish the expression. "Sir?"

Jedric shook his head. "I'll find my own way off. You just get everyone else off this ship."

XVII

KINSKY WATCHED the slowly falling *Spirit Walker* through his binoculars. Pods were dropping from the stateroom deck and engine nacelles and catching up short as parachutes deployed.

He panned up to the top of the ship. "Comrade Admiral! Their crew is bailing out but there's still activity on the flight deck."

Bryndas scowled. "*Forerunner*. Launch fighters. Don't let them get away with that plane!"

In the cockpit of his transport Boyan slid his headset over his ears. He calmly monitored gauges while his engines warmed up as if nothing was amiss, even as the flight deck sank under him. He looked back toward the *Dogoda* and smiled grimly as he saw three small specks drop from its underside hangar bay.

"And in the end, it will have been *your* hand that destroyed the *Forerunner.*"

The needles of his gauges reached the green part of their arcs. He snugged his tie and advanced his throttles.

Lilya's feet danced on the *Forerunner*'s rudder pedals and her hand worked the stick with forced lightness. The deck canted and she locked one brake, fired the opposite engine, and spun the plane around until she could boost back up the incline toward the elevators.

"Come on, Nilo. *Come on . . .*"

The door to the emergency stair flew open and Nilo burst out. For the second time she let out a breath she hadn't realized she had been holding.

Then Jedric dashed out of the stair on Nilo's heels. Her brow shot up in surprise. I guess that will work, she thought, but someone's going to be sitting on someone's lap—

Nilo jumped up on the wing, laid his hand on the latch, and froze.

"Nilo! Get in, for God's sake—"

He pointed across the plane, eyes wide with fear. She spun in her seat and her heart sank as well as she saw the *Dogoda*'s fighters screaming down on them.

She looked back as a thump on the wing marked Jedric's arrival. "You!" she called. "You're a pilot! Combat rated?"

Jedric hesitated. "Yes—no," he answered each question in turn.

Lilya unlatched her seat harness and jumped out. "Get in!"

"Lilya?" Nilo challenged.

But Jedric was already in her seat and strapping in. Lilya leaned back into the cockpit and grabbed him by the lapel of his dinner jacket. "Get my family out of here."

Jedric looked her squarely in the eye. "I will."

Lilya gave her brother a surprisingly calm look. "Strap in, Nilo. Time to go." She turned and leaped off the wing, took two steps toward the stairwell, and turned back long enough to shout, "And Jedric! Watch the Number One converter! It's temperamental!"

Jedric could only nod silently as Armas spooled up the engines.

Nilo watched Lilya dash for the stair until Jedric hit the throttles. The *Forerunner* jerked forward, he fell back into his seat, the hatch slammed shut, and they were off.

Lilya sprinted down the stairs, sliding down rails where she could, leaping over breaks in the catwalks, making her way steadily downward as the *Spirit Walker* gradually came apart around her.

Finally, she reached the bottom level. Down the length of the stateroom deck, past empty rooms' swinging doors, shattered glass, and sliding furnishings pushed into her path by the wind. Through another service door, back into the frame that squealed like a wounded animal as the wind tore it apart from the inside out—

There.

The little fighter plane still hung nestled into its launch rack, right where she had found it the night before. It seemed like an eternity ago. She pulled herself up the gantry into the pilot's seat. It was hard, hanging nose-down over the void, trying to brace herself in the seat while she strapped in, watching the storm-ravaged waves of the gulf looming in her vision getting inexorably closer . . .

She hit the ignition and the engine fired. She reached up to the heavy release handle over her head and jerked, and the plane lurched into free-fall. She flinched as bracing wires snapped dangerously close, but luck was with her and an instant later she was clear of the airship and screaming like a banshee to fight the g-forces as she pulled hard for the sky.

Jedric gingerly worked the *Forerunner*'s controls to get the feel of the unfamiliar ship as he circled over the falling *Spirit Walker*. Inar was half a turn behind him and he eased the plane around, anxiously looking back and forth to spot the fighters.

"Nilo. Armas. Do you see them?"

From his vantage point in the rear cockpit, Armas caught sight of their pursuers, and another craft coming up behind *them*. "I've got them—they're below us, but there's another plane behind *them*."

"Lilya," Jedric confirmed, realizing why she had left. "She found my little toy."

In the mail bay Nilo sank back in his seat, relieved that Lilya had made it, but then was on its edge again. "Armas, what's happening? I can't see anything." He pounded his fist on the tiny window in the mail hatch that was barely useful for letting light in, let alone actually providing a view.

"She's closing on them." Armas watched as Lilya gained a position on the tail of the unwitting trio. Tracers streaked from the nose of her ship and one of the *Dogoda*'s fighters spun down, trailing smoke. "She got one!"

"The Night Witch of the Winter War!" Nilo said to himself.

One of the navy pilots left off his pursuit of the *Forerunner* to engage the new threat, leaving his wingman to continue the chase.

"Jedric!" Armas warned. "Seven o'clock! Use the Surge! Emergency power!"

Jedric obediently flipped up the throttle stops and pushed the levers forward. The engines whined and the *Forerunner* began climbing.

Armas watched the following craft begin to fall behind. Then out of the corner of his eye, a light started to flash yellow. "Oh, no!" he gasped. "Jedric! The Surge! Don't go over fifty-seven percent—"

Just about the time Jedric registered Armas' warning and reached for the throttles the left engine banged and began trailing steam. Their speed faltered and the ship started fluttering erratically.

Jedric put both hands on the stick to keep the unfamiliar craft from spinning out of control. "Armas!" There was an edge of panic in his voice. "You've got that under control back there, right?"

Meanwhile Armas was frantically working switches and valves while simultaneously trying to watch his instruments, while also tracking the fighter plane closing on them. He shook his head to himself and stuck his head down into the mail bay. "Nilo! Get up here and take the gun!"

Nilo squeezed through the conduits and framing members into the rear cockpit, then slipped around Armas as the engineer continued to try to coax their balking engine back to life.

The wind was biting as he opened the canopy and brought the machine gun into position. He ignored the blasting air and drew a bead on the fighter.

When he pressed his thumb to the trigger he was surprised at the recoil. He would have thought the mounting pintle would have kept the gun steady, but the barrel stuttered unexpectedly upward. Nevertheless, small flashes of reflected light marked tearing metal as he clipped the other plane's wing. It wobbled briefly, the panel snapped away, and the fighter rolled sideways and down.

"I got him! Hey, I got him!"

Armas glanced up from his gauges and clapped him on the shoulder, then pointed behind them. "Good! Watch out. There's another!"

Far below the battle, the surging surface of the gulf boiled and three Inar submarines vaulted out of the deep. Hatches flew open and crewmen rushed onto their decks, snapped safety lines into place, and unlimbered flak guns that opened fire on the *Dogoda* and the *Mythos*.

Ahead of the antiaircraft fire, Lilya jinked above the last fighter as it skillfully dodged Nilo's rounds and closed in. This one wasn't like the others, she could tell. This one had skills.

But not enough. She got on his tail, lined up her sights—

Suddenly it was breaking away. She snapped her stick around to follow, but he had an instant's head start on her and was able to disappear into a cloud. She circled back and forth, trying to stay close to the *Forerunner* as it turned back for Inar, while watching for the fighter to reappear, while avoiding the flak bursts from below and tracer fire from the navy ships, all while the lurking carcass of the *Spirit Walker* continued its opera-drama fall from the skies leaving a trail of papers, loose clothes, and debris wafting up in its wake. It was like flying in a confetti machine attached to a steam tractor.

Small wonder, then, when the navy fighter arced out of the top of a cloud, pulled into a dive, and fired a burst into her cockpit.

XVIII

L ILYA'S CANOPY splintered and her instruments erupted into punctured wreckage. Before she could throw up a protective hand, shards of metal raked across her face and she went limp.

In the rear seat of the *Forerunner* Nilo watched in dismay as Lilya's plane nosed over into a dive. "Lilya! She's hit! We've got to help her!"

'We can't!' Jedric's voice on the intercom was urgent, but apologetic. *"We aren't built for that. Hang on!"* Nilo was tossed against the seat harness as the medium pulled hard right to stay out of the gunsight of the navy fighter that was once again sweeping onto their tail.

Then another voice came over the speaker, faint and raspy.

It was Lilya.

"Come in, Forerunner. *Come in . . ."*

"Lilya!" Nilo cried helplessly.

"I read you, Lilya," Jedric answered. *"Go ahead."*

"I'm hit. Losing power . . . have one last burst before the engine goes . . . . Get them out of here, Jedric . . . you promised."

"Lilya!" Nilo shouted.

But now the airwaves were silent.

Lilya clutched one hand to her bleeding left eye and pushed her throttle to the stops. The engine belched smoke and rattled like a scrap grinder but the plane climbed well enough that she was able to get behind the last fighter, who by now was apparently only concerned with his prey and had made the fatal mistake of assuming she was done for.

She was about to convince him otherwise.

Wind whipped at her face through her shattered windshield as she lined her sights up on him. A nudge of the stick, a tap of the pedal, and she pulled the trigger.

Nothing happened.

She pulled it again, and again, and again, but the guns were jammed and refused to fire.

Time slowed. She could almost hear a cheery piano playing in her head, just like when she was the young darling of the crowd scampering out to throw her father's locks with a smile on her face.

Completely helpless, she stared weakly at the plane ahead of her. In that machine a nameless pilot was just doing a job, and when it was all over, if he lived, he would go back to his hangar, climb out with shaking knees, and thank Fate for another day.

Beyond it, the *Forerunner* carried the last people on earth she cared about. She had lost her mother and that had nearly done her in. Now she was about to lose the rest of her family, and there was nothing she could do . . .

Ragged clouds like lily blossoms filled the air in front of her. *No,* she thought. *Not nothing. What else would there be, if she didn't?*

She gunned the engine one last time and it obediently responded. She pulled back on the stick until she was sufficiently high over the other fighter and rolled onto her back.

She swallowed hard, but kept her eyes on her target.

"Goodbye, Papa."

She pulled the nose through the arc into a dive.

Nilo watched with horror as Lilya fell from the sky like a vengeful demon. "What's she doing? Lilya!"

Lilya slammed into the other fighter with a sickening thump. Prop blades chewed aluminum and her target disintegrated into a flaming shower of shredded fragments. Yet her sturdy craft, a testament to its foreign builders, still held its shape even as it continued on, tumbling downward completely out of control.

Thick smoke trailed and the engine finally seized. Something, some fail-safe an anonymous, forward-thinking engineer had thought to incorporate into his new design sensed the random play of g-forces. Maybe it was an inertial switch. Maybe it was an interlock to the engine. Maybe it was simply divine providence on the designer's thought processes. But whatever it was, explosive bolts blew the canopy frame clear and released her seat belts, and Lilya was flung out into the cold air, free of the metal coffin destined for the waters a mile below. As a last valiant act of security for its erstwhile occupant, the plane's fall jerked the static line attached to her harness, releasing her parachute which bloomed white and reassuring above her.

In the back Nilo strained to see her as Jedric arced the *Forerunner* into a tight downward spiral toward her limp form. Something big caught his peripheral vision and he looked up to see the *Dogoda* and its tag-along frigate passing overhead to take up station over the wreckage of the *Spirit Walker,* which had finally completed its collapse and was floundering in heavy waves. The trio of Inar submarines was steaming to engage, sending up a continuous barrage of flak to keep the Reds at bay and allow them to pick up the scattered drop pods and life rafts of Jedric's crew.

Jedric changed frequencies on the radio. "Mayday, mayday, mayday, any Inar vessel," he spoke with forced calm as he continued his orbit of Lilya's parachute. "This is Major Jedric Orianos, Inar Forces Special Services, aboard Soviet aircraft *Forerunner*, over."

The response was immediate. "*This is submarine vessel Silver Wind.*" The excitement in the voice of what must have been a young seaman seeing his first taste of action was clear. "*Go ahead, Captain.*"

Jedric, by contrast, was decidedly sober. "Aircraft damaged. Ditching . . . we have wounded, over."

"*Roger that, sir. Send up a flare. We'll find you.*"

Those simple words were incredibly relieving to Jedric. Not so what came next over the intercom from the rear seat.

"*She's not moving!*" Nilo moaned.

Jedric shook his head to himself. Only one thing at a time! First, he had to get the *Forerunner* down He briefly considered lightening the plane, but the only thing he knew of to dump would have been the gun . . . not enough, and too long to accomplish. No, they were going in as they were.

He turned into the wind as much as he dared. It was pushing up tall waves and he knew if he landed across the swells and hit one on the upside it would be like running straight into a concrete wall.

There would be little need for a rescue flare after *that*.

In the end he lined up his flight path with the bigger waves and crabbed into the stiff breeze. Power on—he would need that for control . . . flaps down for low-speed lift . . . gear up, let her down, down, down; now he could make out the wavelets breaking on the shoulders of the bigger swells that were at eye level—

"Brace yourself!"

They struck the water and skipped over it like a big red stone. The impact jarred Jedric to his teeth, and then they hit again, and again, and finally settled to a sluggish stop in a billowing cloud of steam as the hot engines took on water.

"Armas! Kill the engines!" But the engineer was already on it and they whined down until the only thing he could hear was the blustering wind and hissing steam.

Jedric flung off his harness and jumped out of the cockpit like his old army drill sergeants were coming for him. To his relief he saw Armas and Nilo already at the mail hatch getting Costan out.

Kinsky braced his feet as the *Dogoda* rocked from the shellfire being thrown up from below.

"Submarines, Comrade Admiral. We're taking fire."

Bryndas didn't hesitate. "Ready depth charges."

Kinsky had to admire her. There was no doubt in his mind how she had attained high rank and been given command of the navy's airborne naval forces. The woman was absolutely unshakable.

"Kinsky. Where is the *Forerunner*?

"In the water, Comrade Admiral."

"Put some rounds on it. Make sure there's nothing left."

Despite himself Kinsky was astonished. "But Comrade Admiral . . . it's the *Forerunner* . . . the nuclear motors—"

"Do it!"

Kinsky nodded, wide-eyed, and gave the signal to his gunnery officer. He didn't want to be on the receiving end of another glare like that from the admiral, ever again.

Ever.

Jedric grabbed oars and prepared to pull for the relative safety of the subs as Nilo settled Costan into the raft. Gunfire from the *Dogoda* began to throw up small fountains of foam that walked relentlessly toward them as the airship sought their range.

"Let's go, gentlemen! They're trying to sink the plane!" He looked around. Where was Armas?

There was a building whine and a bigger splash to his left. He looked around to see Armas scrambling from the rear cockpit to the pilot's seat.

"Armas! What are you doing?" He could feel his grip on the situation slipping. "For pity's sake, can't any of you just *escape?*"

Armas reached over the cockpit sill and pushed something. The engines burst into life and blasted steam and spray rearwards. He leaped backward and nearly fell off the wing but managed to find his footing and skipped along the wet metal to the raft and jumped in as the *Forerunner* wallowed away.

Jedric pulled hard on the oars and favored Armas with a cold look.

"What?" the engineer said innocently. "We needed distance!"

Jedric couldn't argue with that. The *Forerunner* was plowing through the rising waves, bobbing over swells and drawing the *Dogoda*'s fire after it.

Armas grabbed a second set of oars and together he and Jedric rowed for all they were worth to where Lilya was still drifting downward. There would be little time to pull her from the water once she hit, and the risk of her being tangled in the parachute and drowning would be high.

If, Jedric thought grimly, she was still alive at all.

Within the *Forerunner*'s cockpit a warning light flashed yellow, then blinked red, then burned a steady baleful brick as a power gauge approached the fifty-seven percent mark, and then snapped beyond.

There was a blinding flash, and a deafening concussion, as the *Forerunner* finally met its fate.

XIX

KINSKY LOWERED his arm from his eyes as the flare faded. Glaring ghost images on his shocked retinas blocked his view everywhere he looked, and it was a few more seconds before he could actually take in the sight of the odd, mushroom-shaped cloud reaching for the storms above that were being shredded by an expanding shock wave.

Then it hit them.

The deck suddenly surged upward. The bridge went dark and static discharges flared from equipment to hapless crew as they were thrown to the floor. Kinsky caught a glimpse of the *Mythos* two hundred meters to their starboard bow as it bore the full brunt of the blast, buckled in the middle, and burst into flame.

"What was that?" He turned to Admiral Bryndas, always steady, always calm . . .

Except this time her face was darkened by the mushroom-shaped shadow, and her eyes were as wide as his.

Armas dared a peek over the gunwale of the raft. "I . . . I . . . ." He swallowed hard. "Was that *full power?*"

Nilo grabbed his shoulder and pointed. "There!"

Lilya dropped the last several feet to the water as the expanding shock wave echoed off distant shores and rebounded at low level, collapsing her parachute. With his priorities refocused Armas joined Jedric and Nilo on the oars and they paddled madly against bobbing waves that threatened to swamp their boat.

Lilya was now floating face-down in the water and wasn't moving. Nilo leaned as far out over the side of the raft as he dared, and Armas dropped his oar and grabbed the boy's belt to give him a few more inches of reach. At last, Nilo's fingers touched Lilya's jacket, snatched hold, and yanked.

"I've got you!"

There was a burble in the water from somewhere around her face and six hands grabbed hold and hauled her, gasping and coughing, into the boat.

Nilo held her face above the sloshing bilge water while Jedric gauged her injuries. With nothing else to do for the moment, Armas dug the flare pistol out of the emergency kit, stood up and fired it into the sky.

He watched the arcing light in comparison to the glowing cloud a few hundred meters away. "You think anyone'll see that?" he asked his companions.

" . . . *Boyan* . . ." Costan whispered in reply.

Armas looked at the old man and shrugged. "You're right. Probably not."

XX

THE DECK of the Inar Republican Navy Submersible *Silver Wind* was not quite awash as the boat skimmed along the surface of the gulf making for home. High overhead the *Dogoda* hung, canted to one side, drifting limply in the fading storm. The mushroom cloud that marked the *Forerunner*'s final resting place by now had reached well above the navy vessel, and its upper reaches were catching the last golden rays of the sunset as reaching tendrils wafted downwind.

Nilo huddled in a blanket forward of the main sail as a medic sat Costan down inside the open aircraft bay to give him some shelter. Lilya was already there, having a bandage fitted over her ruined left eye and shaking her head at the offer of pain medications. Among the injured, Nurse Tatanya moved with purpose, no longer obscured with the persona of a hotel maid.

Armas stood next to Nilo, watching the cloud raptly. "Full power . . ." was all he could mutter, over and over again, to no one in particular. ". . . Full power . . ."

Lilya got up once her wound was tended and came to sit beside Nilo. He looked past her at their father.

"This is it for him, isn't it?" he asked. "He's not any better. We got him out, there's no way you could ever finish Boyan's mission, but he's not any better."

"Who knows if he's even aware of any of that?" She bit her lip when she saw her brother's face. "I'm sorry, Nilo."

He sighed heavily. "It is what it is. You were right. I couldn't fight it. I couldn't make them make it right."

"Are you going to be okay?"

"Okay? I don't know." He fixed his eyes on the deck. "I guess the only question is, can I just take him home? Like this? Or . . . or leave him somewhere?" He wrapped his blanket tighter about his shoulders and seemed to shrink just a little. When he spoke again his voice was small. "It's an impossible choice."

He reached into his jacket pocket and pulled out the damp scrap of newspaper. He peeled it open and read the words.

Lilya— Nilo—Help me!

He felt even more helpless, and he hated it.

He looked around at all the people on the sub's deck . . .his sister, his friend Armas, Jedric (now, he supposed, a 'comrade in arms'), Ursula, the *Spirit Walker*'s crew, even Nurse Tatanya.

No, he thought. Not after all this. Everyone else had done what had to be done. He would as well.

He stood, balled up the clipping, and tossed it to the deck where it skittered toward the impromptu sick bay. "The only way you can make an impossible choice . . . is to change the question."

Lilya looked at him, puzzled.

"Something I heard once from someone," he explained.

"Sounds like they were very wise. Then what is the new question?"

Nilo shrugged, suddenly self-conscious. "Who am I, and what will *I* do? I will take care of him. I *will.* This is where I tip my king and concede." He sat back down and covered his face with his hands. "I guess every son is destined to lose his father someday."

Lilya put her arms around him and squeezed. "Don't worry, Nilo Costanovich. You won't be in this alone."

Jedric stepped past them at that moment on his way toward the aircraft bay and Lilya reached out to stop him.

"Jedric. I owe you an apology."

He stopped, taken aback. "You do?"

"You were right. On the hangar deck."

He nodded slowly as he remembered. "I see." He studied her closely. "Something *is* different now. But you didn't get your apology?"

"I discovered that what I wanted it for, never really happened." Jedric nodded again and looked across the deck to Costan as Lilya went on. "The escape artist could break out of the most elaborate traps but could not free himself of his own grief. And for a long time neither could I. And I couldn't see it."

Jedric squeezed her shoulder in sympathy, stepped past her, then turned back. "Lilya. I have to ask. Why did you give me the plane?"

"Someone had to get them out. You couldn't fly cover."

"But you didn't trust me."

"I still don't."

Jedric's mouth fell open. "I'm sorry?"

Lilya looked him over blandly. "You knew exactly what you were going to do from the moment my father arrived on your ship. You set this all in motion. With a simple suggestion."

Jedric was incredulous. "And yet you put them in my hands?"

"In the end you risked your life to save Nilo, to get him back up onto the flight deck. I thought that should count for something." She turned away to stare at the horizon and the dispersing cloud. "Just don't make me think too hard about it."

The *Silver Wind*'s skipper stepped up to Jedric, but the speechless medium's eyes remained fixed on Lilya. His mouth worked for a moment before words finally came out. "I will make sure I don't!"

The skipper cleared his throat. "Captain? We're in safe waters now."

Jedric pulled his eyes away from Lilya and nodded an acknowledgment to the skipper. He walked the handful of paces back to where Costan sat, laid a hand on the older man's shoulder, and turned to carefully regard the approaching Inar shore. "Things will be better . . . now that we are out of Moroskaya."

He gently lifted his hand.

"In three . . . two . . . *one.*"

Costan shuddered, gasped, and staggered to his feet, rubbing his eyes and looking around anxiously.

"Lilya . . . Nilo . . . where are my children?"

Nilo jumped up, dumbfounded for only an instant. "Papa? . . . *Papa!* We're here! We're here!"

Costan squinted toward the sound of Nilo's voice. "Nilo? Is that—Nilo! My boy . . . my boy!" He reached out, as if still not seeing clearly, as his son dashed across the deck and flung himself into his father's arms.

They embraced tightly and choked back tears until Costan clutched Nilo's face and held him back enough to get a good look at him. "Nilo! My boy! My boy!" He pulled him in close again.

"Papa?"

He looked over Nilo's shoulder and saw Lilya slowly walking toward them.

"Lilya! My angel! You *are* here—"

He faltered when he saw the bandage on her eye and the blood seeping through the gauze. "Lilya . . . my angel . . . what have you been through . . ."

He paused, as if uncertain what to say.

Finally, he managed to find words. "I'm so sorry."

"No, Papa." She held up a hand, and her lip was trembling. "*I'm* sorry. I'm sorry I—"

Costan no longer fought the tears and reached out to pull her in. She threw her arms around his neck, her fists clenched, and sobbed uncontrollably.

After a few moments Costan looked up again and saw Jedric standing apart, waiting patiently as the Campalia family was restored.

Costan suddenly became much more serious. "Major."

"General."

"Are we clear?"

"We are clear, sir."

Nilo looked up, confused, but Lilya eyed her father shrewdly as Jedric, ever the showman, plucked his hopelessly mangled lapel flower from his jacket and flicked it into the gulf.

"All phases . . . are finally complete."

Costan turned slowly and regarded the cloud looming overhead like the smoke of Doom's own furnace. "But the war has come. As we had feared it would."

"You knew they wouldn't let us go easily."

"No, you are correct."

"Papa?" Lilya prompted.

Costan released his hold on his children, took half a step back, and brushed fruitlessly at his jacket. "Well," he managed with forced lightness and a look of embarrassment. "That was a risky venture!"

Nilo looked from Costan to Jedric and back again, and Jedric could see the boy was finally realizing what had happened. What he had done. No—what he and Costan had done *together*.

How they had plotted to get the Campalias out of Moroskaya.

"It was too close for comfort at times, sir, to be sure," Jedric agreed.

Costan put his hands on Nilo's and Lilya's shoulders again and beamed. "But certainly worth the reward!"

Lilya's voice took on a skeptical tone. "Papa? Are you telling me—"

Jedric interrupted quickly. "If I may, sir . . . I would think a greater reward is yet to come." He cocked an eyebrow suggestively.

Costan took the hint. "Yes. Yes, you are correct, Captain."

"Papa!" Lilya demanded. "What is he talking about?"

Costan marked the soggy paper fragment Nilo had discarded. He picked it up, unfolded it, and stared at the writing.

"My little ones. I have . . . a secret. A secret I have kept from you for far too long."

Nilo exchanged glances with Lilya and cleared his throat. "We know, Papa. The, uh, Major told us about you being a spy. Though it sounds more like," and again he looked from Costan to Jedric and back again, "a double agent?"

Costan smiled at his son, but his eyes were still troubled. "No, Nilo. It's not that. Not that at all. Not by half."

"Then what *is* it?" Lilya asked, now sounding completely perplexed herself, again.

Costan looked at the two of them, his expression at once fearful, apologetic, and . . . hopeful.

"Where we're going in Inar . . . Lilya . . . Nilo . . ."

He took a deep breath and plunged ahead.

"Your mother is waiting."

About The Author

Steve grew up on a farm in Northeast Ohio where he spent his free time reading Burroughs, Lovecraft, Zelazny and Tolkien, and his earliest writing efforts were creating adventures for his Dungeons & Dragons group. A veteran of the Army and the Navy, he currently lives near his childhood hometown. He has won awards for his writing in collaboration with Michael Eging on *The Silver Horn Echoes: A Song of Roland*, and has, with Mike, previously published *The Paladin of Shadow Chronicles: Volume One, Annwyn's Blood*, and *Volume Two: Ash and Ruin*.